Dancing the Dream

舞梦

诗与思

【美】迈克尔·杰克逊 ◎ 著

陈东飚 ◎ 译

华东师范大学出版社

Dancing the Dream
舞梦
诗与思
迈克尔·杰克逊

图书在版编目（CIP）数据

舞梦 /（美）迈克尔·杰克逊著；陈东飚译.-- 上海：华东师范大学出版社，2016.1
ISBN 978-7-5675-4706-3

Ⅰ.①舞… Ⅱ.①杰…②陈… Ⅲ.①诗集—美国—现代
②散文集—美国—现代 Ⅳ.①I712.15

中国版本图书馆 CIP 数据核字 (2016) 第036409号

Copyright © 1992, 2016 The Estate of Michael Jackson
Simplified Chinese translation copyright © 2016 by Shanghai Cai Qin Ren Culture Diffusion Co., LTD
This translation published by arrangement with Doubleday, an imprint of The Knopf Doubleday
Publishing Group, a division of Penguin Random House LLC
Through Bardon-Chinese Media Agency
博达著作权代理有限公司
All rights reserved.

上海市版权局著作权合同登记 图字：09-2015-1043 号

Dancing the Dream

舞梦

著　者	［美］迈克尔·杰克逊
译　者	陈东飚
总策划	上海采芹人文化　上海七叶树文化
项目编辑	储德天　陈　斌
审读编辑	许　静
特约编辑	史芳梅　黄　琰
装帧设计	卢晓红　吴元瑛
出版发行	华东师范大学出版社
社　址	上海市中山北路 3663 号 邮编 200062
网　址	www.ecnupress.com.cn
电　话	021-60821666　行政传真　021-62572105
客服电话	021-62865337（兼传真）
门　市	（邮购）电话　021-62869887
地　址	上海市中山北路 3663 号华东师范大学校内先锋路口
网　店	http://hdsdcbs.tmall.com
印刷者	上海中华印刷有限公司
开　本	889×1194　16 开
印　张	12.25
字　数	111 千字
版　次	2016 年 6 月第一版
印　次	2016 年 6 月第一次
书　号	ISBN 978-7-5675-4706-3/J.280
定　价	128.00元
出版人	王　焰

（如发现本版图书有印订质量问题，请寄回本社客服中心调换或电话021-62865537联系）

以挚爱献给

迪帕克[1]

谢谢你的灵感

和你的爱。

[1] Deepak Chopra（1947— ），印度裔美国作家，人类潜能研究与灵体医学专家，迈克尔·杰克逊的多年好友。

前言

每当我听到迈克尔·杰克逊这个名字，我想到的是光芒、眩目的亮星、镭射激光和深沉的情感。我热爱迈克尔·杰克逊。我认为他是全世界最大也最杰出的明星之一，而碰巧他又是全世界有史以来最具天才的音乐制作者之一。

令迈克尔如此独一无二的也许是，无论他获得了多少成就，多少奖赏，这一切都不曾改变他的感性，对他人福祉的关切，或是他对家人与朋友的热忱体贴与爱，尤其是对世界各地儿童的关爱。

我觉得迈克尔就像石蕊纸一样。他总是想要学到更多。他是如此聪明，才华令人惊叹。同时他又非常好奇，想要从留存的人们身上获取养分，历经时光筛选的人们。他真的不属于这颗星球。充盈于他内心的深厚情感创造出了一个超凡脱俗、非同寻常、天真无邪、孩童一般的智者，那就是迈克尔·杰克逊。我觉得迈克尔召唤的是我们所有人内心的孩童，我觉得他拥有我们人人都希望获取或保有的那种天真的品质。

他所拥有的机智极其敏锐，他智慧而又狡黠——用这个词来形容他有点奇怪，因为它意味着欺诈，而他是我一生中所遇见的最无欺诈之心的人之一。他是化身为人的真诚——真诚到痛苦——很容易陷入痛苦的境地。他如此地忘我，有的时候，他只留下非常少的东西来保护那美丽的内心之核，他的精髓。那就是在他身上令我如此热爱，也令全世界真真切切地认同他的东西。

迈克尔·杰克逊，实际上，是无分老幼的国际宠儿，一股不可思议的力，充满了不可思议的能量。在音乐艺术中，他是制作品质的开拓者，高水准娱乐的先锋。什么是天才？什么是活的传奇？什么是天皇巨星？迈克尔·杰克逊——回答完毕。而当你自以为了解他时，他总会给你更多……

我认为他是降临这颗星球的最卓越的人之一，并且，依我所见，他是真正的流行乐、摇滚乐与灵魂音乐之王。

——伊莉莎白·泰勒

舞梦

　　意识通过创造来自我表达。我们活在其中的这个世界是创造者的舞蹈。舞者来来去去仅在一眨眼之间,但舞蹈长存。很多次在我舞蹈的时候,我就已感觉到被某种神圣的东西所触及。在那些时刻,我感觉到我的心灵在飞翔,并与存在的万物合一。我成为星星和月亮。我成为爱者与被爱者。我成为胜者与被征服者。我成为主人与奴隶。我成为歌者与歌。我成为知者与所知。我继续舞蹈下去,那便是创造的永恒之舞。创造者和创造融合成为一个欢乐的完整体。

　　我继续舞蹈而又舞蹈……而又舞蹈,直到存在的唯有……那舞蹈。

——迈克尔·杰克逊

行星地球

行星地球,我的家,我的所在
空间的汪洋大海里一个无常的例外
行星地球,你是否仅仅
飘荡而过,一团尘土的云
一个无足轻重的球,随时会撞成碎片
一小块金属,注定归于锈烂
无意识的真空里一点物质的微粒
一艘孤独的飞船,一颗大个的流星体

冰冷得像岩石一般缺乏色彩
用一点点胶水粘合起来
有一个声音告诉我这不是真的
你是我的甜心,轻柔的蔚蓝色
你是否在乎,你是否占据
一个位置,在我内心情感的最深处
一派温柔,有微风抚慰与充盈
激扬着音乐,萦绕我的灵魂

在我的血脉里我早已领悟
时间回廊的神秘,卷卷史书
年深月久的生命之歌在我血中颤抖
早已舞动过潮水与洪流的节奏
你雾一般的云,你带电的雷暴
曾是以我为形的疾风狂飙

我曾经舔过盐粒，尝过苦与甜
感受每场邂逅，激情，烈焰
你骚动的色彩，你的芳香，你的味道
早已悸动我的感官，超越一切纷纷扰扰
在你的美之中，我已经懂得
永恒至福的法门，当下的这一刻

行星地球，你是否仅仅
飘荡而过，一团尘土的云
一个无足轻重的球，随时会撞成碎片
一小块金属，注定归于锈烂
无意识的真空里一点物质的微粒
一艘孤独的飞船，一颗大个的流星体

冰冷得像岩石一般缺乏色彩
用一点点胶水粘合起来
有一个声音告诉我这不是真的
你是我的甜心，柔和的蔚蓝色
你是否在乎，你是否占据
一个位置，在我内心情感的最深处
一派温柔，有微风抚慰与充盈
激扬着音乐，萦绕我的灵魂

行星地球，蔚蓝色的温柔
我爱你，用我心中的所有

第

魔法之子

曾经有一个孩子,他自由不羁
在内心深处,他感觉欢笑
喜悦与自然天性的游戏
他不曾被来世的念头困扰
美和爱是他所见的全体

他知道他的力量是上帝的力量
他如此确信,他们觉得他很反常
这天真的,同情的,光的力量
威胁着祭司们并造成了一场恐慌
千方百计他们总想要否弃
这股他们无法掌控的神秘原力

千方百计他们企图消灭

这孩子始终在神恩中沐浴
他从不为时间或地点所禁锢
在五光十色的梦里,他嬉闹游戏
表演自己的角色,他呆在永恒里

预言家一个个跑来卜算
有的危言耸听,有的则妄言
诟病这孩子,这令人迷惑的精灵
他与世上的其他人毫无共性
他是真的吗?如此的怪诞
他不可预知的天性没有框限
他让我们如此困惑,他是否坦诚?
他的目标是什么?什么是他的命运?

而当他们窃窃私语,暗中谋划
通过无尽的谣言来把他拖垮
要杀死他的神奇,将他恣意踩躏
烧毁他的勇气,令他的恐惧倍增
那孩子依旧是那么简单,真诚

他想要的只是山的高度
为云着色,描画天宇
他要飞翔,超越这所有的疆域
在天地造化之中,永不死去

不要阻止这孩子,他是人之父
不要挡他的路,他是命定之数
我就是那孩子,但你同样是如此

你只是忘记了，只是失了端倪

在你心中坐着一个先知哲人
在他的思绪之间，他侧耳倾听
一曲，简单却又奇妙地清晰入微
生命的音乐，那么珍爱，那么宝贵

倘若你能够在一瞬间了然
这创造的火花，这精微的光焰
你便会前来与我共舞
点起这堆火来让我们目睹
这个地球上所有的孩童
编织他们的魔法，将新生递送
给一个自由的世界，没有苦怨
一个欢乐的世界，更加健全

内心深处，你知道这就是真相
快找到那个孩子，他就藏在你身上。

没有我的翅膀

那是八月,我正仰望着天空。一只手罩着我的双眼,我辨出一只猎鹰翱翔在炽热的涡漩气流之上。它盘旋着越飞越高,直到随着一声超乎凡尘的尖啸,而消失不见了。

一时间我有了被抛弃之感。"为什么你没有我而长出翅膀?"我悲叹道。随后我的灵魂说道:"猎鹰的路并非唯一的路。你的思想跟任何鸟儿一样自由。"于是我闭上眼睛,我的灵魂便起飞了,盘旋得像猎鹰那么高继而更超乎其上,这样我便是在俯瞰整个地球了。但似乎有点不对劲。为什么我感觉这么冷,这么孤单?

"你长出翅膀却没有我,"我的心说道,"没有爱的自由又有什么用?"而我静静地走到一个病童的床前唱一支摇篮曲给他听。他微笑着入睡了,于是我的心腾飞而起,加入我的灵魂,它就在地球的上空盘旋。我自由而有爱了,但还是有点不对劲。

"你长出翅膀却没有我,"我的身体说道,"你的飞行仅仅是想象。"于是我检索起了我以往曾经无视的书籍,阅读每一个时代里真正会飞的圣人。在印度、波斯、中国,还有西班牙(甚至在洛杉矶!),灵魂的力量所抵达的不只是心,更是进入身体的每一个细胞。"仿佛被一只巨鹰带上了云霄,"圣女大德兰①说,"我的迷醉将我托举到半空。"

我开始相信这惊人的技艺了,并且第一次,我没有了被抛弃之感。我就是那猎鹰和孩童和圣人。在我的眼中他们的生命变得圣洁,而真理到家了:当一切生命都被视为神圣,人人都会长出翅膀。

---

① Saint Teresa(1515-1582),罗马天主教圣人,伽尔默罗会修女。

生命之舞

我躲不开月亮。它柔软的光束推开夜的窗帘。我甚至不必看见它——一束凉而又蓝的能量碰到我的床,我于是起身。我奔过黑暗的厅堂把门甩开,不是要离家而是要回身走进去。"月亮,我在这里!"我喊道。

"好,"她回答,"现在给我们来点舞蹈吧。"

但我的身体在她说任何话之前很久就已经动起来了。什么时候开始的?我不记得了——我的身体一直在动。从儿时起我对月亮就是如此反应,身为她最爱的疯子,而且不只属于她。星星将我拉近,足够靠近这样我才能将它们闪烁的行为看个究竟。它们也在跳舞,在做着一种轻柔的分子摇摆,令我的碳原子和着拍子跳动。

我甩开双臂,朝大海奔去,它在我体内唤起又一支舞。月亮的舞蹈舒缓于内,轻柔如草坪上蓝色的影子。当浪涛涨满,我听见地球的心跳,节拍加速。我感觉到海豚在白色的泡沫中腾跃,想要飞,几乎就在飞,当波浪高高翻卷上天的时候。它们的尾巴留下光的弧线如同波浪中闪烁的浮游生物。一群小鲶鱼升起,亮银在月光里闪耀仿佛一个新的星座。

"啊!"大海说,"现在我们快要聚起一大帮了。"

我沿着海滩奔跑,一脚追逐波浪另一脚躲避它们。我听见微弱的爆音——一百只惊惶的螃蟹正钻进自己的洞里,以防万一。但我此刻正在疾行,一会儿踮着脚尖,一会儿全速飞奔。

我扬起我的头,一片飞旋的星云说:"赶快,打转!"

咧嘴一笑,我低下头来保持平衡,尽我所能狂野地旋转起来。

这是我最爱的舞蹈,因为其中有一个秘密。我转得越快,我体内就越是静止。我的舞蹈唯动于外,唯静于内。无论我多么爱做音乐,永不死去的还是那听不见的音乐。而宁静就是我真正的舞蹈,尽管它一动不动。它伫立一边,我优雅的编舞者,祈福每一个手指和足趾。

此刻我已忘却了月亮和大海和海豚,但我却置身它们的欢乐之中犹胜以往。像一颗星星一样远,像一粒沙子一样近,那所在者升起,微光闪烁。我可以置身其中直到永远,它如此可爱与温暖。然而一旦触碰到它,光便从那静止中激射而出。它令我颤栗与悸动,我知道我的命运就是向别人呈现这宁静、这光芒、这至福就是我的舞蹈。我接受这个礼物只为将它再次送出。

"快点,送出去!"那光说道。

从未经历过,我试图照做,发明新的步点、新的欢乐姿态。突然间我意识到我的所在之处,便回身奔上山去。我的卧房的灯亮着。看见它我就回复了平静。我开始感觉到我怦然而动的心,我双臂中的睡意,我双腿流动的热血。我的细胞想要舞得慢一些。"我们能稍走几步吗?"它们说,"有点太狂野了。"
"当然。"我笑道,减速成为一种松弛的慢步。

我转动门把,轻喘着,很高兴有了疲惫之感。爬回到床上,我回想起某件我一直弄不明白的事。他们说我们抬头看见的星星有些并不在那里。它们的光要用几百万年抵达我们,我们所做的一切只是凝望着往昔,望着一个早已逝去的,那些星星依旧能够闪耀的时刻。
"那么一颗星星不再闪耀之后又做什么去了?"我问自己,"也许它就死了吧。"
"哦不,"我头脑中一个声音说,"一颗星星是永远不会死的。它只是变成了一个微笑,重新融入到宇宙的音乐、生命之舞里面去了。"我喜欢这个念头,我双眼闭上之前的最后一个念头。带着一个微笑,我自己也回身融入到音乐中去了。

当婴儿微笑

当梦者在梦中亲吻他们的所爱
而彩虹编织并抛洒它们的色彩
那些时刻鲜活得如此夺目
我们孤注一掷,纵身跃入
深渊之内
我们被悬停了片刻
那些都是婴儿微笑的时刻。

那些都是命运启封的时刻
无物不可能,我们的伤已愈合
我们可以飞,我们可以翱翔
在火上行走,在天空中巡航
藉着一颗亮星的光照
没有距离,万物都咫尺之遥
那些都是天真狡诈的时刻
光辉之下
我们被悬停了片刻
那些都是婴儿微笑的时刻。

那些时刻心脏变得柔软
当海景在瑰丽壮阔中闪现
当天堂的笑声回荡凡尘
而我们在重生之中焕然一新
在一场超越时光的永恒里
怀着天使间的兄弟情谊

我们翻滚与欢畅

我们灵魂的游乐场

幽暝之中

我们被悬停了片刻

那些都是婴儿微笑的时刻。

那些时刻我们与上帝合一

万物皆善，无物怪异

在默然的冥想之间

我们感觉到我们的完满

我们就是源头，我们就是熔炉

无物能伤及我们，因为我们不可征服

没有罪，没有罪人

我们唯有胜利，我们已感到一线光明

福佑之中

我们在此飘游片刻

那些都是婴儿微笑的时刻。

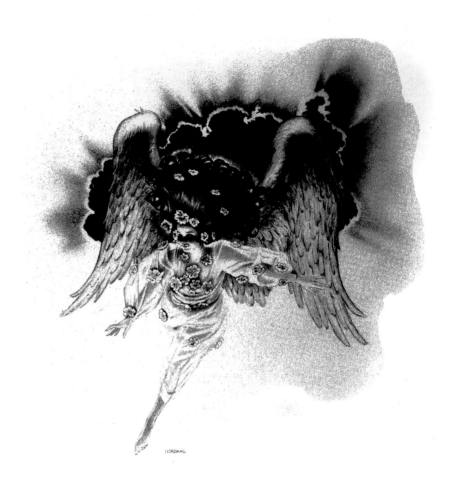

王国颠覆，丧失其等级

文明崩塌，世代流逝

疾风暴雨将重重大海倾翻

残忍的屠戮，无视我们的申辩

可露滴依旧闪烁，孩子玩耍

暴君们哭泣，无物可供戕杀

仙女跳舞，妖精歌唱

人皆加冕，人皆为王

在花园里

我们嬉戏片刻

那些都是婴儿微笑的时刻。

但心说不

他们看到穷人住在纸板窝棚里,于是他们就把窝棚推倒来造工程。大块的水泥和玻璃高耸在沥青的停车场之上。不知怎的它不太像家,即使是窝棚里的家。"你指望什么呢?"他们不耐烦地问,"你们太穷,不可能像我们一样生活。除非你们可以为自己做得更好,你们应该心怀感激,不是吗?"

脑袋说是,但心说不。

在城市里他们需要更多的电,于是他们找到了一处山溪来建水坝。随着水位上升,死兔死鹿就漂过来了。太小还飞不了的幼鸟在巢中溺毙,母鸟无助地哀鸣。"这不好看,"他们说,"但是现在一百万人整个夏天都可以开空调了。这比一条山溪更重要,不是吗?"

脑袋说是,但心说不。

他们看到一个遥远国度的压迫与恐怖主义,于是他们对其发动战争。炸弹令那个国家化为瓦砾。它的人民在恐惧中退避,每天都有更多的村民在粗糙的木棺里下葬。"你必须准备好作出牺牲,"他们说,"如果有些无辜的旁观者受了伤,那不正是人们必须为和平付出的代价吗?"

脑袋说是,但心说不。

岁月滚滚而过,他们变老了。坐在他们舒适的住宅里,他们清点账目。"我们这辈子过得很好,"他们说,"而且我们做了正确的事。"他们的子孙低眉,问为什么贫穷、污染和战争仍未解决。"你们很快就会发现,"他们回答,"人类软弱而又自私。哪怕我们再尽力,这些问题也永远不会真正结束。"

脑袋说是,但孩子们凝视自己的心低声说道:"不!"

全世界的孩子

全世界的孩子,我们会做到的
我们会在无尽的海滩相聚
造起沙堡,荡起我们的船
当人们争斗不休,固守己见
永远戴着新做的面具
我们会摇撼时间的潮水来做到。

全世界的孩子,我们会做到的
用歌用舞和天真的祝福
还有一个爱之吻的轻抚
我们会做到的。

当商人交易,为价格斤斤计较
而政客们如此刻意地友善
我们会在无尽的海滩相聚,荡起我们的船
我们会做到的。

当律师争论,医者行医
证券经纪人给肉报价
当传道者传道,摇铃
投机客有东西出售
我们会在天真的祝福中歌舞
用一个爱之吻的轻抚
我们会做到的
在无尽的海滩上相聚
造起沙堡,荡起我们的船
我们会做到的。

我们会乘上彩虹,云朵,雷霆
飞翔在风中,我们会变形
我们会触摸星星,拥抱月亮
我们会冲破藩篱,瞬间抵达

当建筑师将大楼设计得高耸入云
而工会提升嚎叫的音量
当董事会议室的口角产生热度
而商家在秘密场所里会晤
我们会在天真的祝福中歌舞
用一个爱之吻的轻抚
我们会做到的。

当哲学家苦思,继续破解
身体与心灵无尽的两难
物理学家彷徨,继续冥想
空间与时间永恒的诘问
考古学家勘测,继续挖掘
大大小小的往世宝藏
心理学家摸索,分析泪水
是来自谵妄之念,恐慌,忧惧

当牧师们听取忏悔
在一个严肃的时段
而人与人争斗
在纷乱与嘈杂之间
在聒躁与喧嚣之间
纠结罪恶的意义
我们会触摸星星,拥抱月亮
冲破藩篱,瞬间抵达
乘上彩虹,云朵,雷霆
飞翔在风中,变形

全世界的孩子,我们会做到的
用歌舞和天真的祝福
一个爱之吻的轻抚
我们会做到的。

于是大象继续前行

关于大象有一个奇怪的事实是这样的：为了活下去，它们绝不可以倒下。其他每一种动物都可以绊倒了又再爬起来。但一头大象总是站立着，即使是睡觉。如果象群里面有一头滑倒了，它就没救了。它侧身躺着，一个自身重量的囚徒。尽管别的大象会悲伤地聚拢在它周围并试图将它再抬起来，但它们通常是无能为力的。随着呼吸的缓慢起伏，那倒地的大象会死去。其他的伫立守候，然后慢慢地继续往前走。

这是我从自然书籍里学到的东西，但我怀疑它们对不对。大象不能倒下难道没有另一个原因吗？也许它们打定了主意不这样做。不倒下是它们的使命。作为最聪明也最耐心的动物，它们定了一个协议——我想象那是亿万年以前，在冰川时代快结束的时候。大群大群地横越地球的表面，大象最早窥见了小个子的人类潜行于高草之间，手持他们燧石的长矛。

"这种生物有什么样的恐惧和愤怒啊，"大象思索，"但他必将继承地球。我们聪明得足可以看清。就让我们给他树立一个榜样吧。"

于是大象将它们灰白的脑袋凑到一起沉思。它们能给人类展示什么榜样呢？它们可以向他展现它们的力量比他大得多，因为那是确定无疑的。它们可以在他面前显示它们的愤怒，可怕得足以将整座森林连根拔起。或者他们可以用恐怖来主宰人类，践踏他的土地，碾碎他的棚屋。

在万般沮丧之际，野象会干出所有这些事来，但聚成一群，把脑袋凑到一起时，它们决定人类从一个更和善的信息中或许可以学得最好。

"让我们向他呈现我们对生命的尊重吧。"它们说。而从那天起，大象便始终是沉默、耐心、和平的生物了。它们让人类骑乘它们，给它们套上鞍辔就像奴隶一样。它们允许孩子们哂笑它们在马戏团里的把戏，更被逐出它们曾经作为主宰生活过的非洲大平原。

但大象最重要的信息是在它们的运动之中。因为它们知道活着就是运动。黎明复黎明，岁月复岁月，象群不断前行，一大群从不倒下的生命，一支不可阻挡的和平大军。

天真的动物，它们毫不疑心终究会有这一次，它们将成千上万地倒在一颗子弹之下。它们会躺在尘土里，被我们无耻的贪婪所残害。巨型的雄象最先倒下，这样它们的长牙便能制成小饰物了。随后倒下的是母象，这样人们就可以拿到战利品了。幼象尖叫着奔逃远离它们亲生母亲的鲜血气味，但从枪口逃离对它们毫无用处。默默地，因为没有照料者，它们也一样会死去，它们的尸骸会在阳光下化为白骨。

在这么多死亡之中，大象只要放弃即可。它们要做的全部就是颓然倒地。那就足够了。它们不需要子弹：自然已经给了它们躺下来安息的尊严。但它们记得它们古老的契约和它们对我们的誓言，那是至高无上的。

于是大象继续前行，而每踏一步都在尘土里扬起词语："观看，学习，爱。观看，学习，爱。"你能听见它们吗？在羞愧中的某一天，一万个原野之王的魂灵会开口说："我们不恨你们。难道你们到头来还看不到吗？我们愿意倒下，这样你们，亲爱的小个子，就再也不会倒下了。"

男孩和枕头

一个聪明的父亲想要给他的小儿子上一堂课。"这是一只枕头,上面盖着绸缎,里面填有大地之上最稀有的鹅绒,"他说,"到城里去看看它能换来什么。"

男孩先去到市场,在那里看到一个有钱的羽绒商贩。"你愿意给我什么来换这个枕

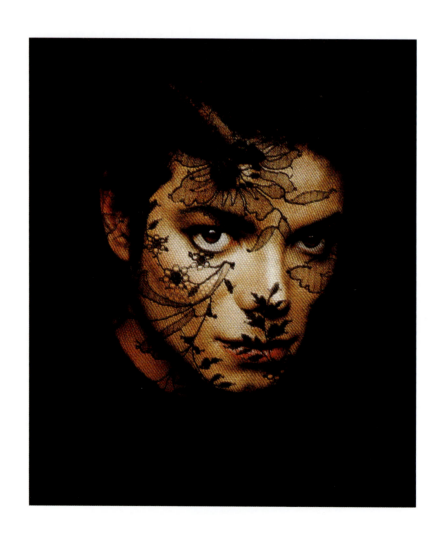

头?"他问道。商贩眯缝起眼睛："我会给你五十个达克特[①]，因为我看这确实是一件稀罕的宝贝。"

男孩向他道了谢，继续朝前走。随后他看到一个农妇在路边叫卖蔬菜。"你愿意给我什么来换这个枕头?"他问道。她摸了它一下就叫道："多柔软啊！我愿意给你一块银币，因为我好想把我疲乏的脑袋搁在这样一个枕头上面。"

男孩向她道了谢，继续朝前走。最后他看到一个年轻的乡下女孩在清扫一座教堂的台阶。"你愿意给我什么来换这个枕头?"他问道。带着奇怪的微笑看了看他，她回答道："我会给你一分钱，因为我看你的枕头跟这些石头比起来太硬了。"丝毫没有犹豫，男孩把枕头放到她的脚下。

回到家里，他对父亲说："我给你的枕头寻到了最好的价钱。"接着他掏出了那一分钱。

"什么?"他父亲叫道，"那个枕头至少值一百达克特呢。"

"那是一个有钱的商贩眼里看到的，"男孩说，"但因为贪婪，他给我的出价是五十。我得到了一个比那更好的出价。一个农妇出价给我一个银币。"

"你疯了吗?"他父亲说，"什么时候一个银币比五十个达克特值得更多了?"

"当它是因爱而出价的时候，"男孩回答，"如果她给了我更多，她就不会有钱来养她的孩子了。不过我又得到了一个比那更好的出价。我看见一个乡下女孩在清扫一座教堂的台阶，她给我的出价就是这一分钱。"

"你已经完全不可理喻了，"他父亲说道，摇着头，"什么时候一分钱比一个银币值得更多了?"

"在它是因虔诚而出价的时候，"男孩回答，"因为她是在为她的主而劳动，他的屋宇的台阶看来比任何枕头都更柔软。比最穷的人还要穷，她仍有时间来尊奉上帝。这就是我把枕头交给她的理由。"

对此聪明的父亲报以微笑并拥抱了他的儿子，眼含着泪水他喃喃说道："你学得很好。"

[①] Ducat，中世纪欧洲的金币或银币。

今天到此为止

舞蹈排练可以持续超过午夜，但这一次我十点就停了。"我希望你不介意，"我说道，望向深空，"但今天到此为止。"

一个声音从控制室里传来："你没事吧？"

"有点累，我猜。"我说。

我披上一件防风夹克，朝大厅走去。奔跑的脚步在我身后跟来，我非常确定它们属于谁。"我太了解你了，"她说道，追上了我。"到底是什么问题？"

我犹豫了一下。"呃，我不知道这听上去怎么样，但我今天在报纸上看到一张照片。一只海豚溺死在一张渔网里面。从它的身体被绳线缠住的样子，你能读出那么多的痛苦。它的眼睛空洞，却还留着那道微笑，海豚从来不会失去的微笑，即使在它们死去的时候……"我的声音逐渐减弱。

她把她的手轻轻放在我的手上："我知道，我知道。"

"不，你还不知道全部。我不只是感到难过，或是必须面对一个无辜生命已经死去的事实。海豚爱跳舞——在所有的海洋生物里，那是它们的标志。对我们一无所求，它们在波浪中腾跃让我们惊叹。它们疾驰在船舶之前，不是为了第一个抵达而是要告诉我们，'一切就是为了游戏。保持你的航向，但你要一边跳舞一边走。'

"这就是我的念头，在排练当中，我想到，'他们是在杀死一支舞蹈。'那时候好像就应该停下来才对。我无法阻止一支舞蹈被杀死，但至少我可以在记忆中暂停，像一个舞者对另一个舞者那样。这有没有道理？"

她的目光温柔。"肯定的，从某种意义上说。很可能我们还要等很多年，大家才会对怎样解决这事达成共识。涉及到那么多的利益。但等待明天的进步太让人困惑了。你的心现在就想要发言。"

"是的，"我说，为她推开房门，"我就是有这感觉，今天到此为止。"

古人的标记

他在沙漠里生活了一辈子,但对我来说一切都是新的。"看见沙子上的脚印吗?"他问道,指着悬崖边的一个点。我尽力细看。"不,我什么也看不到。"

"问题就在这里。"他笑道,"你看不到一个印记的地方,那正是古人曾经行走的地方。"

我们走得更远一点,他又指了指一处开口,在一道沙石墙壁的高处。"看见上边那间房子吗?"他问道。我使劲眯起眼睛:"什么也看不见。"

"你是个好学生。"他微笑道,"没有屋顶或烟囱的地方,就是古人极有可能生活过的地方。"

我们拐了一个弯,眼前铺开的是一片不可思议的风景——成千上万朵沙漠的花朵绽放着。"你能看到少了什么吗?"他问我。我摇摇头:"就只是一波又一波的美好。"

"是的,"他用低沉的嗓音说道,"什么也不缺的地方,就是古人收获最多的地方。"

我思索着这一切,思索着曾经与地球和谐共生,不留任何标记以损伤他们所居之地的一代代人。那晚在营地里我说道:"你遗漏了一件事。"

"是什么?"他问道。

"那些古人都埋葬在哪里?"

并不答话,他用自己的棍子捣火。一道明亮的火焰蹿起,舔食空气,然后消失。我的导师瞥了我一眼问我是否领悟了这一课。我一动不动地坐着,我的沉默告诉他我已领悟。

治愈世界

在你心里有一个地方
我知道它就是爱
这个地方可以更加光明
比明天更亮
如果你真的努力尝试
你会发现无需哭泣
这个地方我感觉没有伤与悲

有很多路通向那里
如果你对生者足够关心
腾出一点点空间
造一个更好的地方
治愈世界
把它变成一个更好的地方
为你也为我
也为了人类全体

多少人正在死去
如果你对生者足够关心
造一个更好的地方
为你也为我

如果你想知道为什么，有一种爱不会撒谎
爱很强大，它只关心快乐的给予
如果我们努力尝试，我们会看见
在这份祝福里我们感觉不到
惶恐或惧怕

那就让我们停止苟存而开始生活
这样就永远感觉得到
有爱就足够让我们生长
造一个更好的世界
造一个更好的世界
治愈世界
让它变成一个更好的地方
为你也为我
也为人类全体

多少人正在死去
如果你对生者足够关心
造一个更好的地方
为你也为我

而那个曾经孕育了我们的梦
会显现它欢乐的面庞
而那个我们曾经相信的世界
会在神恩中重新闪耀

那我们为什么执意将生活扼杀
伤害这地球，折磨它的灵魂
尽管这本是一目了然
这世界宛如天堂
我们可以是上帝的荣光
我们可以飞得那么高
让我们的精神永不死去

在心里我感觉你们都是我的兄弟
创造一个世界没有恐惧
在一起我们流下欢乐的眼泪
好让所有的国度把刀剑变成犁铧
我们真的可以抵达那里
腾出一点点的空间
来造一个更好的地方
治愈世界
让它变成一个更好的地方
为你也为我

还有人类全体

多少人正在死去
如果你对生者足够关心
造一个更好的地方
为你也为我
治愈世界
让它变成一个更好的地方
为你也为我
还有人类全体

多少人正在死去
如果你对生者足够关心
造一个更好的地方
为你也为我

治愈世界
让它变成一个更好的地方
为你也为我
还有人类全体

多少人正在死去
如果你对生者足够关心
造一个更好的地方
为你也为我

多少人正在死去
如果你对生者足够关心
造一个更好的地方
为你也为我

多少人正在死去
如果你对生者足够关心
造一个更好的地方
为你也为我
为你也为我
为你也为我
为你也为我
为你也为我
你也为我
你也为我

孩子们

孩子们在他们游戏的微笑中向我呈现人人皆有的神性。这单纯的善从他们的心中直射光芒。这里面有那么多的教谕。倘若一个孩子想要巧克力冰淇淋,他就开口来要。成年人则因纠结于是吃还是不吃冰淇淋而凌乱。一个小孩唯享受而已。

我们需要在孩子身上学到的东西并不孩子气。跟他们在一起让我们与生命的深层智慧相连接,它无时不在,只要求你身体力行。现在,当世界如此混乱而它的问题又如此复杂之时,我觉得我们比任何时候都更需要我们的孩子。他们天生的智慧指出解决之道,它就在那里,等候着被辨认出来,就在我们自己的心里。

母亲

亿万年时光延续我的妊娠
在百转千回中化为一形
源自于无明这包容宇宙的孕育
是这地球上一场不可思议的接纳
随后在一个注定的八月早晨
从你的存在之中我降生了
用温柔的爱你哺育一粒种子
对自身的苦痛你毫不留意
不在乎一切险阻与危难
你为这孤独的陌生人打定了主意

彩虹，云朵，深蓝的天空
闪闪发光，展翅高飞的鸟儿
从碎片之中你将我拼合成一体
你用诸般元素打造我的灵魂
亲爱的母亲，你给了我生命
因为你，没有倾轧或争斗
你给了我欢乐与立身之所
无条件地对我悉心关怀
而倘若我有一天会改变世界
那正是源自你所开启的情感
你的慈爱之心如此甜蜜与宝贵
你最纤细的情感我也听得见
我能领悟你最微小的念头
你的爱之灵丹那奇妙的魔法

而此刻我已经走了这么远
见过了每一个国王与沙皇
邂逅了每一种色彩与每一种
激情的信条，每一种贪婪
我回到那个星光煜煜的夜晚
毫不恐惧强力与强权
是你教我如何挺身来战斗
为了每一种不公与正义
日复一日地坚持毫无保留
我会珍视你所铸造的一切
我会记住每一个亲吻
你甜蜜的词语我永远不会遗忘
无论我由此动身去往何处
你在我的心里，我亲爱的母亲。

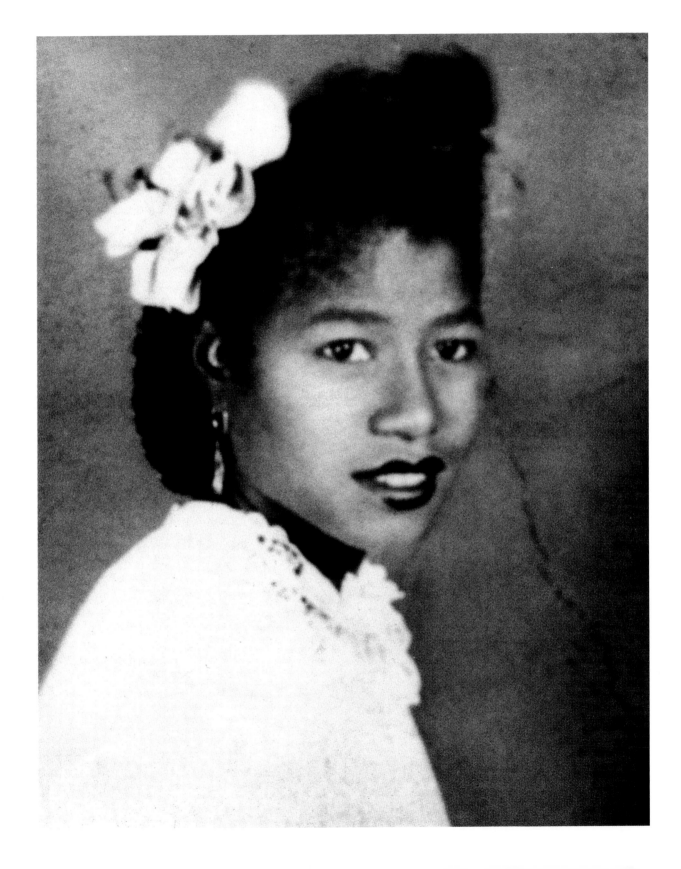

魔法

我对魔法的观点跟舞台上的把戏和幻象没什么关系。整个世界充满了魔法。当一条鲸鱼跃出海面像一座新生的山峰,你会在始料未及的喜悦中大口喘息。什么样的魔法啊!但一个学步幼童看见他的第一只蝌蚪闪现在一洼泥塘里时也会感觉到同样的震撼。惊奇充满了他的心,因为他在一瞬间窥见了生命的游戏。

当我看见云朵疾掠远离一座雪冠的山峰,我就直想要大喊:"太棒了!"自然,一切魔法师中的佼佼者,传递了又一个震撼。她已显现了真正的幻象,我们被她的奇观所震惊的无能。每一次太阳升起,自然都在重复着一个命令:"看呐!"她的魔法无限奢华,而作为回报我们要做的一切就是欣赏它。

自然必定会感到的是何等的喜悦啊,当她用涡旋的气体和虚无的空间造出星辰。她抛掷它们像晶亮的饰物飞出一袭天鹅绒斗篷,给我们十亿个理由在纯粹的欢乐中醒来。当我们敞开心扉来欣赏她已经给予我们的一切,自然便找到了她的奖赏。喝彩之声滚过宇宙,她便鞠躬还礼。

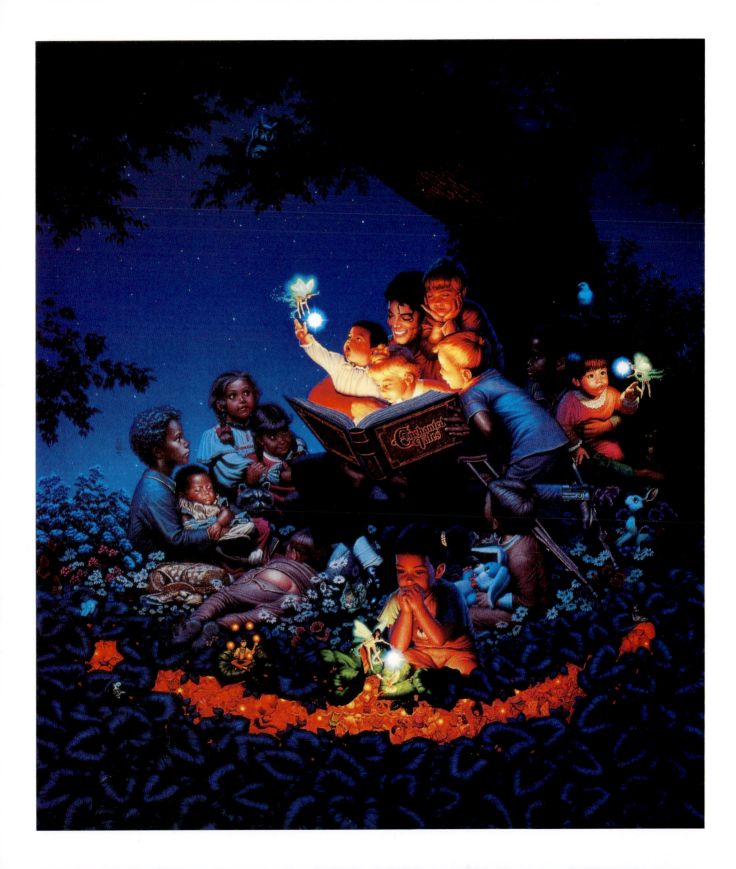

口渴的鱼

　　一天夜里一条幼鱼正睡在某个珊瑚丛下面,上帝现身在他的梦中。"我要你动身去送一个信给海里所有的鱼。"上帝说道。
　　"我该告诉他们什么呢?"小鱼问道。

"只要告诉他们你口渴了，"上帝回答，"再看他们会做什么。"随后再无一言，他便消失了。

第二天早晨小鱼醒来回忆起了他的梦。"上帝要我做的是一件多么奇怪的事啊。"他自忖道。但当他一看见一条大金枪鱼游过，小鱼便高声呼叫起来："抱歉，我口渴了。"

"那么说你一定是个傻瓜。"金枪鱼说。轻蔑地一甩尾巴，他游开了。

小鱼的确感觉有点傻，但他有命令在身。他看到的下一条鱼是一条龇着牙的鲨鱼。保持一段安全的距离，小鱼喊道："抱歉，先生，我口渴了。"

"那么说你一定是疯了。"鲨鱼回答。注意到他眼中一股颇为饥饿的神情，小鱼迅速游开了。

整整一天他遇见了鳕鱼和马鲛鱼和剑鱼和石斑鱼，但每次他作出自己的简短演讲，他们便背转过身，不想与他扯上干系。感觉无可救药的困惑，小鱼找到了海里最睿智的生物，正巧是一条老年的蓝鲸，他的身侧有三道鱼叉的伤痕。

"抱歉，我口渴了！"小鱼叫道，疑心这条老年蓝鲸连看都看不到他，他是那样一个小不点儿。但那智者在他的路径上停下了。"你看见过上帝了，对不对？"他说。

"你怎么知道的？"

"因为我也曾经口渴过。"年老的鲸鱼笑道。

小鱼眼中充满了惊奇。"请告诉我上帝的这个信息是什么意思。"他恳求道。

"它的意思是我们寻找他找错了地方，"年老的鲸鱼解释说，"我们为寻找上帝而上下求索，但不知怎的他并不在那里。于是我们责备他，对自己说他一定是把我们遗忘了。不然我们就断定他很久以前就离开了我们，即使他曾经来过。"

"多么奇怪啊，"小鱼说道，"想念无所不在的东西。"

"非常奇怪，"年老的鲸鱼赞同道，"这是否让你想起说自己是口渴的鱼呢？"

天真

很容易把天真误认为是头脑简单或是幼稚。我们都希望显得见多识广；我们都希望显得精明世故。天真就是"跳出来"。

然而在天真之内有一个深刻的真理。一个婴儿望着他母亲的双眼，他所见的全都是爱。当天真消褪，更复杂的事物便取而代之。我们认为我们需要智胜他人并设下计谋来获取我们想要的东西。我们开始花费大量的精力来保护自己。随后生命就变成了一场争斗。人们别无选择唯有变得精明世故。否则他们又如何生存呢？

当你专注一心的时候，生存意味着将事物看成它们真正所是的样子并作出反应。它意味着开放。而那恰恰就是天真。它简单而又轻信就像一个孩子一样，不擅加判断而执着于一个狭隘的观点。如果你被禁锢在一种思维与反应模式里面的话，你的创造力便会受阻。你会失去当下一刻的新鲜感与魔法。要学会再一次变得天真，那新鲜感才永不消褪。

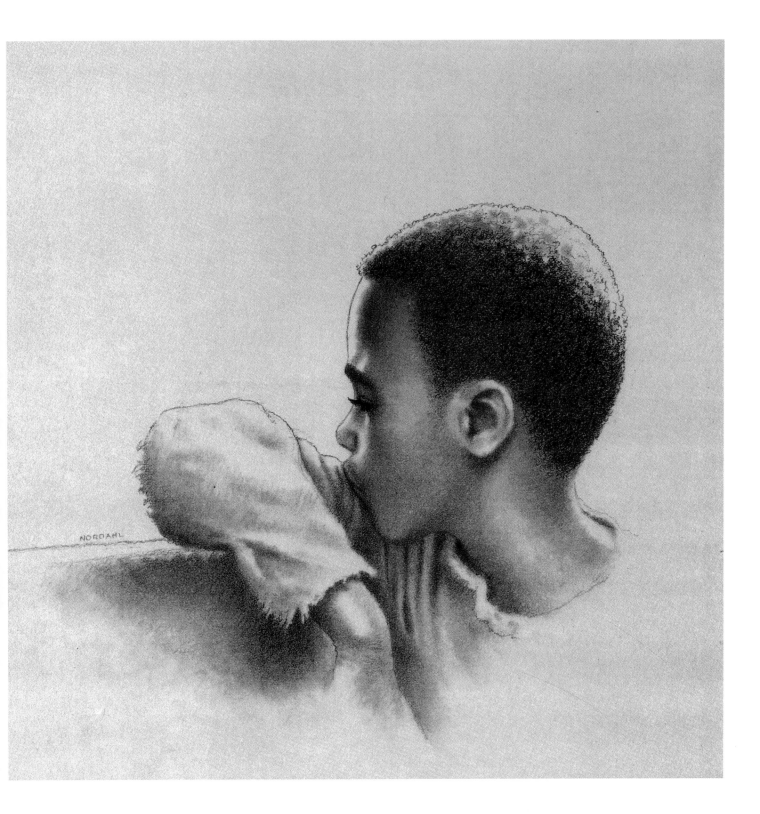

信任

我在公园里喂松鼠的时候,注意到有一只小的似乎并不信任我。其他的都凑得足够近来吃我手里的食物,他却保持着距离。我朝他丢去一颗花生。他慢慢靠拢过来,紧张地抓住它,就跑掉了。下一回他必定不那么害怕了,因为他稍微凑近了一点。他越感到安全,他就越是信任我。最后他干脆坐到了我的脚下,像任何吵闹着要下一颗花生的松鼠一样胆大。

信任就像那样——它永远是仿佛一步步地信任你自己。别人无法替你克服恐惧;你必须自己做到才行。这很难,因为恐惧和怀疑总是抱得很紧。我们害怕被抛弃,害怕再一次受到伤害。于是我们保持一段安全的距离。我们认为将自己与其他人分隔开来会保护我们,但那同样是无效的。它只让我们感觉孤单而不被人爱。

信任你自己始于认识到害怕是可以的。心怀恐惧并不是问题,因为人人都会在某些时候感到焦虑和缺乏保障。问题在于做不到足够的诚实来承认你的恐惧。无论何时我接受了我自己的怀疑和不安全感,我都会对他人更加开放。我越深入我自身,我就变得越强大,因为我意识到我的真实自我远远大于无论什么样的恐惧。

通过完全接受你自己,信任变得完全。再没有了任何人间的分隔,因为再没有了任何内心的分隔。在曾经盘踞着恐惧的空间里,爱的生长已获得准许。

勇气

很奇怪，究竟什么需要勇气，什么又不需要。当我迈步走上舞台面对成千上万人的时候，我并不觉得我很勇敢。向一个人表达真情实感可能需要更多的勇气。当我想到勇气时，我想到的是《奥兹的巫师》①里的胆小狮子。他总一见危险就逃。他经常哭叫，因恐惧而发抖。但他也和他的所爱分享自己的真情实感，即使他并不总是喜欢那些情感。

那需要真正的勇气，亲密的勇气。表达你的情感跟在别人面前崩溃并不一样——它是接纳并忠实于你的内心，无论它会说什么。当你具有亲密的勇气时，你知道你是谁，你也愿意让别人看到。这很吓人，因为你感到如此脆弱，如此易于被拒绝。但没有自我接纳，那另一种勇气，英雄们在电影里展示的那种，就显得空洞了。无论有多少风险，诚实与亲密的勇气都打开了自我发现的路。它呈现的是我们全都想要的东西，爱的承诺。

---

① The Wizard of Oz，即《绿野仙踪》，根据美国作家鲍姆（L. Frank Baum, 1856–1919）的儿童小说《奥兹的神奇巫师》（The Wonderful Wizard of Oz，出版于 1900 年）改编并多次翻拍的电影、音乐剧等。

爱

爱是一件描述起来很滑稽的事。它那么容易感觉却又那么难以捉摸而无从谈论。就像浴缸里的一块肥皂——它就在你的手中，直到你握得太紧为止。

有的人花费了一生在他们自身之外寻找爱。他们认为必须将它紧抓不放才能拥有它。但爱却滑走了，就像那块肥皂一样。

把握爱并没有错，但你必须学会轻轻地把握它，抚弄一般。它想飞时就让它飞。当它被允诺了自由时，爱便是让生命活跃、欢乐、崭新的事物。它是激发我的音乐、我的舞蹈、所有一切的汁液与能量。只要爱在我心里，它便无所不在。

上帝

很奇怪，上帝并不介意在全世界的所有宗教里表达他/她自己，而人们却依旧紧抓着唯己之道方为正道的观念。无论你试图谈论有关上帝的什么，总有人会受到冒犯，即使你说每个人对上帝的爱对于他们自己都是正确的。

对于我来说上帝所取的形并非最重要的事。最重要的是那精髓。我的歌和舞只是轮廓，让他前来填满。我将形献上，她将甘甜注入。

我曾仰望夜空，注视如此亲密地近在咫尺的星辰，就好像它们是我的祖母给我做的一样。"多么丰富，多么奢华。"我想到。在那一刻我看见了上帝现身于他的造物之中。我也可能同样轻易看见她在一道彩虹的美、一只鹿跃过一处草坪的优雅、一个父亲之吻的真诚之中。但对我来说与上帝最甜蜜的接触是无形的。我闭上眼睛，向内观看，便进入一片幽深轻柔的宁静里。上帝之造物的无限将我拥抱。我们是一体。

我怎样做音乐

人们问我怎样做音乐。我告诉他们我只不过是迈步走进去。就像是迈步走进一条河加入到水流中去。河中的每一个刹那都有自己的歌。于是我便待在这刹那里倾听。

我听到的从来不会千篇一律。穿过树林的一次漫步带来一支噼啪作响的轻歌：树叶在风中飒响，鸟儿叽喳，松鼠叱嚷，细枝在脚下吱嘎碎断，我的心跳将这一切汇拢。当你加入到水流中去，音乐在内也在外，两者是一回事。只要我能倾听这刹那，我便永远会有音乐。

瑞安·怀特①

瑞安·怀特，正义的象征
或天真的孩童，爱的信使
你现在哪里，你去了哪里？

瑞安·怀特，我想念你的阳光之日
我们无忧无虑畅玩着漫长的游戏

我想念你，瑞安·怀特
我想念你的微笑，天真又明亮
我想念你的荣耀，我想念你的光

瑞安·怀特，矛盾的象征
反讽的孩童，还是虚构的孩童？

我想到你分崩离析的生活
想到你的奋斗，想到你的抗争

当女士们在月光照耀的夜里跳舞
包租游轮上正举行香槟酒会

我看见你的颓唐之形，你幽灵般的目光
我感觉到你溃烂的伤口，你备受摧残的瘀痕

瑞安·怀特，愤怒与痛苦的象征
无名恐惧化为癫狂的象征
在一个歇斯底里的社会
其中满是飘游不定的焦虑
和伪装的虔诚

我想念你，瑞安·怀特
你向我们显示如何站起身来战斗
在雨中你曾是一场欢乐的倾洒
每个女孩和男孩心里希望的迸发

在你苦恼悲伤的深处
曾经是另一个明天的梦

---

① Ryan Wayne White（1971–1990），美国一患血友病的少年，因输血感染爱滋病而被逐出就读的中学，在旷日持久的诉讼之后得以重返学校。瑞安·怀特的抗争得到了政治、文化、艺术各界诸多名人的支持，成为全国性事件，极大地改变了人们对于爱滋病的认知，以及美国政府与社会对爱滋病人关怀的状况。作为瑞安·怀特的主要捐助人和生前好友，迈克尔·杰克逊曾以《太早离去》（Gone Too Soon）一曲纪念他的逝世。

抓不住的影子

即使我旅行得再遥远
我灵魂的门依旧半开半掩
身陷于死亡恐惧的纠缠
你的音乐我不曾听见
穿过记忆小巷里曲折的路径
我背负着十字架忍受苦刑

那是一段疯狂的行旅
是悲哀中生出的万般痛楚
我上上下下徘徊
畏缩逃避每一场挫败
寻找那被窃走的玉露琼浆
我心中那失去已久的权杖
这些面孔一张张满布忧愁
我在其中寻找我的绿洲

某种意义上那是一次醉后癫狂
一场残忍的瘾症，一片雾霭迷茫
多少次我曾试图将它打破
这影子跟着我怎么也甩不脱
多少次在嘈杂的人群之间
置身于如此喧响的忙碌与纷烦
我朝身后窥看它的踪迹
无论在哪我都无法将它丢弃

只有当我摆脱了所有的桎梏
在尖声哭喊的静谧之后
在那些起伏的叹息的深处
那想象中一千个谎言的悲苦
突然间我凝望你炽热的瞳仁
我找到了我的目标，就在这一瞬
那抓不住的影子就是我的灵魂

关于全世界的孩子

我们必须治愈我们受了伤的世界。我们今天所见的混乱、绝望、无意义的破坏，都是人们对于彼此和所处环境的疏离之感造成的。这种疏离的根源往往来自一个情感上贫困的童年。孩子们已被偷走了童年。一个孩子的心灵需要神秘、魔法、惊奇还有兴奋的滋养。我希望我的作品帮助人们重新发现藏在自己内心的孩子。

两只鸟

很难告诉他们我对你是什么感觉。他们从来没有见过你,谁也没有你的相片。那么他们怎么才能理解你的神秘呢?我们给他们一条线索吧:

两只鸟栖在一棵树上。一只吃樱桃,另一只瞭望。两只鸟飞过空气。一只鸟的歌声落下有如水晶从天空中落下,另一只保持沉默。两只鸟在阳光中打转。一只鸟的银色翅膀触到了光,而另一只则张开隐形的翅膀。

很容易猜到我是哪只鸟,但他们永远不会找到你。除非……

除非他们已经懂得了一份永不干涉、从彼处观望、在隐形的空气中自由呼吸的爱。甜蜜的鸟儿,我的灵魂,你的沉默是如此的可贵。要有多久世界才会在我的歌里听见你的歌?

哦,那是我渴望的一天!

最后的眼泪

你的言词捅进我的心，我流下痛苦的眼泪。

"出去！"我吼道，"这是我这辈子为你而流的最后的眼泪。"于是你走了。

我等了几个钟头，但你没有回来。那一夜我独自流下了困惑的眼泪。

我等了几个星期，但你没有话要讲。想着你的声音，我流下了寂寞的眼泪。

我等了几个月，但你没有给我留下任何讯息。在我心深处，我流下了绝望的眼泪。

多么奇怪，所有这些眼泪都洗不掉那伤痛！随后一份爱的思念刺穿了我的怨恨。我回想起你在阳光下，挂着五月的酒般甜美的微笑。一滴感激的眼泪开始落下，这时奇迹般地，你回来了。柔软的手指触摸我的脸颊，你为一个吻而俯身。

"你为什么来了？"我低声说。

"为了抹掉你最后的眼泪，"你回答，"那是你为我保留的一滴。"

迷醉

我生而永不死去

要活在至福之中,永不哭泣

要说真话而永不撒谎

要分享我的爱而无一声哀叹

要伸开我的臂膀而无一丝羁绊

这是我的舞,这是我的高点

不是一个秘密,难道你看不见

为什么我们不能全都活在迷醉里

迷醉　　迷醉

为什么我们不能全都

活在迷醉里

没有一份负疚,没有悔恨

我在此地要忘却

想象之罪那被玷污的记忆

在每个朋友、相识与亲属身上

我们已经来到此地庆贺

摆脱了来自每一种观念的

每一种恐惧,每一粒种子

无论属于哪种分裂、等级,或教义

这疏远,破碎,憎恶

来自分裂,剥削,孤立

这残忍，歇斯底里，绝对的疯狂
这愤怒，焦虑，满溢的悲伤
被破坏的生态，恣意的毁灭
染病的生物学，自然的阻碍
濒危的物种，环境的污染
臭氧层里的洞，蔑视解决
并不知道那照亮我内在的火花
是同一把火，闪耀在每个男人、孩子、至高的母亲

我们已经来到此地庆贺
摆脱了来自每一种观念的
每一种恐惧，每一粒种子
无论属于哪种分裂，等级，或教义。

感觉到自由，让我们起飞
进入浩瀚无界，比天空更远
因为我们生而永不死去
要活在至福之中，永不哭泣
要说真话而永不撒谎
要分享我们的爱而无一声哀叹
要伸开我们的臂膀而无一丝羁绊

这是我们的舞，这是我们的高点
不是一个秘密，难道你看不见
为什么我们不能全都活在迷醉里

迷醉　　迷醉
为什么我们不能全都
活在迷醉里。

柏林 1989

他们恨这堵墙，但他们又能怎么样？它太过强大根本无法洞穿。

他们怕这堵墙，但那不是顺理成章的事么？很多想要翻过它的人都被杀害了。

他们不信任这堵墙，但又有谁不是这样？他们的敌人拒绝拆除一块砖，无论和平谈判拖到多久。

墙冷笑道："我是在给你们一个很好的教训。"它夸口说，"如果你们要为永恒而建造，别用石头费事了。仇恨、恐惧、不信任要强大得多。"

他们知道墙是对的，他们几乎就要放弃了。只有一件事阻止了他们。他们记得谁在另一边。祖母，表兄，姐姐，妻子。渴望被看见的亲人的脸。

"什么事？"墙问道，颤抖着。对自己做了什么一无所知，他们正把这堵墙看透，试图找到他们至爱的亲人。沉默中，从一个人到另一个人，爱始终在做着它看不见的工作。

"停下！"墙尖叫道，"我要倒了。"可是太晚了。一百万颗心已经找到了彼此。墙在倾颓之前已经倒掉了。

地球母亲

一个冬日，我正沿着海滩在走。低头俯视，我看见一道波浪将一枚羽毛推到沙上。那是一枚沾着油污的海鸥羽毛。我将它拣起来，用我的手指感触它黝黑润滑的膜。我禁不住疑心这鸟是否幸存了下来。它在那儿还好吗？我知道它并不好。

我悲伤地想到我们对待我们的家园是多么漫不经心。我们所有人共有的地球不止是一块抛过太空的石头，而是一个活的、养育一切的生命。她关心我们；她理应得到我们关心的回报。我们一直以来对待地球母亲的方式就像某些人对待一间出租公寓一样，就是先糟蹋再搬走。

但现在并没有地方可以搬去。我们已将我们的垃圾、我们的战争和我们的种族主义带到了世界的每一部分。我们必须开始清扫她，而这意味着首先清扫我们自己的心灵与头脑，因为是它们引导我们毒害了我们亲爱的星球。我们改变得越早，越是容易感受我们对地球母亲的爱和她如此慷慨地回赠给我们的爱。

聪明的小女孩

我认识一个聪明的小女孩,她不会走路。她被禁锢在一辆轮椅上,她也许会在那上面度过余生,因为她的医生们对让她瘫痪的双腿有任何改善几乎已不抱希望了。

当我第一次遇见这个小女孩时,她向我亮出一个微笑,用它闪耀的欢乐点燃了我。她如此地敞开心怀!她并未因自怜而躲藏,或是请求认可,或是出于一份羞耻感而自我保护。她对于无法行走的感觉是完全的天真,就像一只小狗对它是混种还是冠军血统一无所知。

她对自己不作任何判断。这是她的智慧。

我在其他孩子脸上见过同样聪明的表情，社会眼中的"可怜"孩子，因为他们缺少食物、金钱、安全的家，或健康的身体。到某个年龄的时候，这些孩子里很多人就会了解到自己的处境有多糟。成年人看他们的生活的眼光夺走了他们如此可贵而又稀有的最初的天真。他们开始相信他们应该对自己感觉很糟；相信那是"对的"。

但这个聪明的小女孩，只有四岁，却飘浮在怜悯与耻辱之上像一只无忧无虑的麻雀。她把我的心捧在手上，令它如一片棉絮般没有重量，使得我甚至没有可能想到："多可怕的事啊。"我所见的一切都是光明和爱。在他们的天真之中，非常小的孩子们知道自己就是光明和爱。如果我们允许的话，他们可以教会我们同样地看待我们自己。

来自一个小女孩凝望之中的一个火花，容纳了自然在每一种生命形式的心中植入的同一种知识。那是生命的无声秘密，不可形诸言语。它就是知道。它知道平和，知道如何不去伤害。它知道即使最细微的呼吸也是一个对造物主感激的动作。它微笑而活，耐心地等待着世世代代的无知与悲伤像一道蜃景般逝去。

我看见这知识在孩子的眼中越来越多地呈现自身，这让我想到他们的天真正变得越来越强大。他们终将解除我们成年人的武装，而那也终将足以解除世界的武装。他们感觉不到破坏环境的理由，于是环境便会毫无争议地被清扫干净。一个聪明的小女孩告诉了我未来，在她望着我的时候，如此充满了平和与满足。我为信任她胜过所有专家而欣喜。当光明与爱驱走我们的罪孽与耻辱，她的预言必将成真。

我你我们

我对你说你必须这么做。你说你不愿意。我们商谈这件事,然后我们达成共识说也许我可以帮忙。

我说你错了。你坚持你是对的。我们握住彼此的手,对错便消失了。

我哭了起来。你也哭了起来。我们拥抱,而在我们之间开出了一朵和平之花。

我多爱这个名叫"我们"的谜啊!它从哪儿来的,是从稀薄的空气里么?我思索这个谜,我意识到了什么:"我们"必定是爱的宠儿,因为除非我向你伸出手来,"我们"甚至都不存在。它乘着温柔的翅膀而至;它通过我们无声的默契说话。当我笑我自己时,它微笑。当我宽恕你时,它欢腾起舞。

于是"我们"便不再是一个选择,倘若你和我愿意彼此在一起成长的话就不是。"我们"令我们合而为一,倍增我们的力量;它扛起我们的重担,在你和我准备好让它落下来的时候。真相是你和我本来早就要放弃了,但"我们"不会让我们这么做。它太聪明了。"直视你们的心,"它说,"你们看到了什么?不是你和我,而只有'我们'。"

光的天使

很难看到天使,尽管我凝视着他们的图画已有好几个钟头。有人不用图画也能看见他们,而且他们会讲有趣的故事。守护天使全都是女性,例如,我当初发现这点时并没有吃惊。一个诞生天使,从年轻的等级中招募来的,照料每个婴儿出生的时候,而另一个天使,较为年长但并不阴沉,帮助临死的人离开这个世界而没有悲伤或苦痛。

你可以向天使祈祷,他们会倾听,但召唤他们的最好方式,有人告诉我,是笑。天使会回应欢乐,因为那是造就他们的材料。事实上,当人们的心思被愤怒或仇恨蒙蔽的时候,没有哪个天使能找到他们。

不是所有天使都有翅膀——幻想家们声称是这样——但有翅膀的可以展开一大片金色的羽毛铺满整个世界。如果你的双眼可以直视太阳的话,你会看到一个无可抗拒的天使在那里统辖着一切;一个更沉静的则从月亮的表面发出微笑。

天使终其一生,也就是永远,都围绕在造物主的王座周围,唱着他的颂歌。有灵敏耳朵的人们曾经听到过。天使合唱团的和声复杂得不可思议,他们说,但韵律却很简单。"基本上就是进行曲的拍子。"一个偷听者证实说。出于某种原因,这几乎是迄今为止我听过的最好的一件事。

一段时间后就有点寂寞了，光是听说天使的事，却不能亲眼看见。当一个看天使的人听到这事的时候，她震惊了。"看不见吗？"她说，"但你心里就有一个天使啊。人人都有。我现在就能看到它，我想你也可以的。""不，"我伤心地说，问它长得什么样，"它看上去像我吗？"

"呃，又像又不像，"看天使的人神秘地回答说，"那都取决于你认为你是什么样。你的天使是一个光点栖息在你心灵的正中心。它比一个原子还小，但是等等看。一旦你接近了它，你的天使就会变大。你越是靠近，它就变得越大，直到最后，在一道光的闪耀里，你会看到你的天使真正的原形，而恰恰就是在这一个刹那，你也会看到你自己。"

所以我现在一直都在寻找我的天使。我静静地坐着，将我的凝视转向内心。不久我便瞥见了某样东西。"是你吗，天使，拿着一支蜡烛？"一声扑翅然后便消失了。然而那已经足以让我的心狂跳起来了。下一回我的天使将会挥舞着一盏灯，然后是高举着一个火把，然后是点着一个火堆。

那是看天使的人所保证的，既然我已见过了荣光，我的所知便足以相信。

我曾寻找我的星星

小时候我曾经在夜里仰面躺在草地上。我开始把星星一颗一颗区分开来,希望其中有一颗可以是我的,像一个想象的朋友。

最初我挑的是北极星,因为它是一个孩子最容易找到的,一旦你看明白那个大勺子就快要兜住它的时候。但我希望我的星星是一颗会动的星星,而不是这样一颗恒星。此外,海上的水手会迷路的,如果没有北极星指引他们的话。

随后我在天鹅座的心里挑出了两颗特别的星星。所有其他的星星看上去都是白的——但这两颗是明亮的蓝色和金色。它们让我想起成对的珠宝,但在我可以选择之前,我停了下来。它们彼此拥有,只拿一个一定很不公平。

猎户座的腰带有一瞬间令我注目,但我不是一名猎手。我最好也别去碰天狼星,任它的鼻子紧追天体的踪迹,它的尾巴猛击着天空。

最终我转向了我的最爱,七姐妹。对我来说她们就像装束整齐要赴舞会的淑女一样,

裹在一层薄纱般的青云之中。但谁会忍心把这七姐妹拆散呢？

我的游戏教了我很多有关夜空的事，但我已渐渐长大。拥有我自己的星星的整个念头消失了，很难回忆我最后究竟有没有选中一个。人们开始告诉我"星星"这个词指的是某样截然不同的东西。我对他们半信半疑，然后有一夜我在床上辗转反侧，苦恼而又焦虑。我的心在困扰中感觉沉重。挣扎着站起身，我望向窗外。浓厚的层云遮蔽了午夜的天空。没有星星！

我不寒而栗，想到一个没有星星的世界。水手在海上没有了可以信赖的指引，没有了珠宝眩闪我们的美感，没有猎手指向下一道地平线，没有可爱的女郎循香奔赴天空的舞会厅。但在地球四围，空气如此肮脏，城市的灯火如此明亮，对一些人来说再也看不到什么星星了。一代儿童可能会看着一块空空如也的天空长大而发问："那儿有过星星没有？"

让我们把它们还给天空，让我们现在就去做——在为时太晚以前。我将会寻找我的星星直到我找到为止。它就躲在天真的抽屉里，裹在一条惊奇的披巾里面。我会需要一张星图来告诉我它会填满哪个洞，而那会是一个小洞。但在地球上我们有五十亿个人，我们全都需要天空。找到你的星星把它扔到天空上去吧。你仍旧拥有它的，不是吗？

一个孩子就是一首歌

当孩子们听音乐时,他们不只是听。他们溶化到曲调里,跟着旋律流动。里面有什么东西开始展开它的翅膀——很快孩子和音乐便合而为一了。我也是那样感觉的,在音乐面前,而我创造的最佳时刻经常是和孩子们一起度过的。当我在他们周围的时候,音乐便走向我,像呼吸那么容易。

每首歌都是一个由我哺育并给予爱的孩子。但哪怕你从未写过一首歌,你的生命就是一首歌。它怎么可能不是?一波接一波,自然轻抚着你——每一个黎明和每一个日落的旋律是你的一部分,飘落的雨触摸你的灵魂,而你也会在跟太阳玩捉迷藏的云团里看见你自己。活着就是音乐飞扬,从你血管里舞蹈的血液开始。一切活的事物都有一首旋律。——感觉每一首,轻柔而又专注,便可引出它的音乐。

你有没有感觉到你的音乐?

孩子们感觉得到,可一旦我们长大了,生命便成为一个负担和一件琐事,而音乐则越来越微弱。有时心会如此沉重,以致我们对它背转身去,忘了它的悸动乃是生命最智慧的信息,一个无言的信息,它说的是:"活吧,存在吧,动吧,欢乐吧——你是活的!"没有心的智慧旋律,我们不可能存在。

当我开始感觉到一点点疲惫或负荷过重时,是孩子们将我唤醒。我转向他们寻找新生,寻找新的音乐。两只褐色的眼睛那么深邃地望着我,那么天真,而在内心我低语道:"这孩子是一首歌。"那是一份如此真实与率然的体验,刹那间我再次领悟:"我也是一首歌。"我又一次重回了我自己。

天真之子

天真之子,我想念你阳光灿烂的日子
我们在漫长的游戏中欢乐嬉闹
自从你离开了这一片风景
街道便寂寞,黑暗,而又卑劣

天真之子,现在回到我这儿来
带着你简单的微笑让他们看
这世界怎样才能又一次回应你的眼光
而心跳和着你舞蹈的旋律扑动

天真之子,你的优雅,你的美
此刻在使命的召唤以外向我呼叫
来和我一起远走高飞
越过爱之国度的重重山脉

天真之子,欢乐的信使
你毫无一丝机巧便触到我的心
我的灵魂在一场狂妄的火中燃烧
改变这世界是我最深的欲望

你会在那儿吗?

抱住我就像约旦河一样
于是我会对你说
你是我的朋友
带着我就像你是我兄弟
爱我就像一个母亲
你会在那儿吗?

疲惫时告诉我你会抱住我吗?
犯错时你会淬炼我吗?
迷惘时你会找到我吗?
可他们告诉我一个人应该有信念
无能为力时也迈步
战斗到最后
可我只是凡人

人人都想要控制我
仿佛世界有一个角色给我
我如此迷惑
你会不会引导我
你会在那儿等我
足够在乎而给我支撑?

抱住我,让我看到
低下你的头
轻轻地,勇敢地

带我到那儿
我只是凡人

抱住我,让我看到
低下你的头
轻轻地,勇敢地
带我到那儿
我只是凡人

带着,带着
勇敢地带着我
轻轻地,慢慢地
带我到那儿
我只是凡人

揉捏我
爱我,喂我
吻我,释放我
我就会感到幸福

孤独中
当我寒冷而又孤独
需要的只有你
你还会在乎吗?
你会在那儿吗?

救我
治愈我，沐浴我
轻轻地你对我说
我会在那儿
可你会在那儿吗？

抱住我
搂着我，佑护我
触摸我，治愈我
我知道你在乎
可你会在那儿吗？

孤独中
当我寒冷而又孤独
（我有时会孤独，我会孤独）
而需要的只有你

你还会在乎吗？
你还会在那儿吗？

带着
勇敢地带着我
轻轻地，慢慢地
带我到那儿

揉捏我
爱我，喂我
吻我，释放我
我就会幸福

呼唤我
救我，面对我

祝福我，对我说
我会在那儿
我知道你在乎

救我
治愈我，沐浴我
轻轻地你对我说
我会在那儿
可你会在那儿吗？

喂我
喂我，抚慰我
当我孤独而又饥饿
你还会分享吗？
你还会在乎吗？

看护我
抚慰我，别离开我
当我苦痛，流血
瘀伤而又赤裸
你还会在乎吗？

吻我
面对我，吻我
而当我的心正破碎
你还会在乎吗？
你会在这儿吗？

举起我
小心地把我举起来
我在疲惫中倒下
我知道你在那儿
可你还会在乎吗？

第 2 部分

有魔法的孩子

有魔法的孩子曾经感到一下刺痛
一段模糊的往事，一段零乱的回忆
在色彩、形状、色调里
似乎有一个谜，一丝难辨的线索
在风、暴雨、狂飙的背后
裹着尸衣，被面纱遮掩
在一种奇妙的图案中隐而不见
似乎有一股他无法彻悟的力量
它的音乐和节奏嬉闹而又甜蜜
他在它怦动的节拍中幸福地舞蹈
冷还是热他都不介意
高山之巅是他的君王宝座

陌生人跑来轻看他的欢乐
用嘲弄与哂笑他们想要毁掉
他们心目中一场高明的游戏
用残忍的枪矛他们想要夺走
扼杀，窒息他天真的神奇
奋力反抗，无视他们的愚妄
一次又一次要窃走他的雷霆
无视他们的攻击，他们打不垮
用他们所有的倒刺，他们抢不走

上帝的爱之赠予，他们伪装不了
不懂他的力量或他在寻找什么
他们大声抱怨，称他为怪胎

但那神秘的力却始终坚持
有魔法的孩子变得无畏而勇敢
纵身跃入他的灵魂深处
在至高的迷狂中他发现了自己的角色
在他的自我中是无限的疆域
这神秘的力是人类的希望
穿透那存在的面具
在那超越一切视觉的沉默里
是一片田野，它有不一样的故事
一片充满力量、非凡荣光的田野
有别的孩子在里面，如果将它开启
它的浪潮定会将世界改变

有魔法的孩子已准备好要弯下腰
播撒种子，抓起犁锄
不费吹灰之力，不叹一口气
不流一滴眼睛，不发一声哭泣
用无声的完美
跟从上帝的指引
一起歌唱，就像一个种族
阻挡那潮水，改变这地方

有魔法的孩子，别担心怎么做
不要耽搁，就是现在这一刻。

你在听吗?

我是谁?

你是谁?

我们从哪里来?

我们到哪里去?

这一切是怎么回事?

你有没有答案?

不朽是我的游戏

我从至福中来

我在至福中得到支撑

我向至福回返

如果你现在不知道

真是可惜

你在听吗?

我的这副身躯

是一团能量之流

在时间之河里

亿万年过去,世代往复

我出现又消失

玩着捉迷藏

只在一眨眼之间

我是粒子

我是波浪

以闪电的速度旋转
我是起伏波动
独领风骚
我是王子
我是小丑
我是行动
亦是完成
我是星系，宇宙的真空
在银河之上
我是热狂

我是思索者，思索，思想
我是追寻者，追寻，被追寻者
我是露滴，阳光，风暴
我是现象，田野，形式
我是沙漠，海洋，天空
我是原初的自我
在你和我之中

纯粹无界的意识
真理，存在，至福是我
在无限的表达中我来而复去
玩着捉迷藏
只在一眨眼之间
但不朽是我的游戏

亿万年过去
在内心深处
我依然
始终如一
我从至福中来
我在至福中得到支撑

加入我的舞蹈
请即刻加入我
如果你忘了自己
你永远不会知道怎样
玩这个游戏
在永恒大洋的底层

停止这希望的苦楚
把它玩尽
别去想，别犹豫
在你的内心弓身向后
只要创造……只要创造

不朽是我的游戏
我从至福中来
我在至福中得到支撑
我向至福回返
如果你现在不知道
真是可惜
你在听吗？

破茧而出

这一切歇斯底里,这一切纷繁骚乱
时间,空间,能量只是一个理念
我们形诸概念的东西全都是自创的
所有被爱的,所有被恨的

何处是开端,何处是终点
时光的箭,要弯折是多么难
那些背弃了的承诺,它们究是何义
那些爱的信笺,从未投递

我们曾在那里

先于开端，先于狂暴
先于被打破的沉默之苦恼
一千个渴望，从未表达
悲伤的剧痛，被残忍地扼杀

但我已选择挣脱，要自由驰骋
切断那些束缚，好让我见证
那些把我囚禁在痛苦记忆中的枷锁
那些搅乱我头脑的责难、解说

那些溃烂难除的伤口已消失不见
取而代之的是一场新生已初现
那孤独的孩子，依旧抓着自己的玩具
已创造了他的和平，发现了他的乐趣

在没有时间的地方，不朽显露
在爱充满的地方，没有恐惧
这孩子已经长大来编织他的魔术
抛却他不幸的人生，曾是何等悲剧

他此刻，已准备好随时去分享
随时去爱，随时将关怀送上
打开他的心，没有任何保留私藏
现在加入他吧，如果你有胆量

天堂在此

你和我从未分离
那只是一个幻象
制造它的魔法透镜名叫
感知

只有一种完满
只有一个心思
我们就像涟漪
在意识的汪洋大海里

来吧,让我们跳起
创造之舞
让我们庆贺
生命的欢乐

飞鸟,蜜蜂
无限的星空
河流,山岭
云层和峡谷
都是一个脉动的样式
活着,呼吸着
注入了万物能量的生机
充满了生命,欢乐
这一个我的宇宙
不要害怕

要知道你是谁

你远不只是

你曾经的想象

你是太阳

你是月亮

你是盛开的野花

你是生命的悸动

起伏不停，舞蹈

从一点微尘

到最遥远的星辰

而你和我

从未分离

那只是一个幻象

制造它的魔法透镜名叫

感知

让我们庆贺

生命的欢乐

让我们跳起

创造之舞

在我们内心弓身向后

我们创造

一次又一次

无尽的循环来了又走

我们欢乐

在时间的无限之中

从来没有过一个时间
我不存在
或你不存在
从来不会有一个时间
我们会停止存在

无限　　无界
在意识的汪洋大海里
我们就像涟漪
在至福之海上

你和我从未分离
那只是一个幻象
制造它的魔法透镜名叫
感知

天堂在此
当下就是永恒的
那一刻
别愚弄你自己
快拿回你的至福

你曾经迷失
但现在你到家了
在一个非定域的宇宙里
无处可去
从这里到这里

是无界的

意识的汪洋大海

我们就像涟漪

在至福之海上

来吧,让我们跳起

创造之舞

让我们庆贺

生命的欢乐

并且

你和我从未分离

那只是一个幻象

制造它的魔法透镜名叫

感知

天堂在此

当下,永恒的这一刻

别愚弄你自己

快拿回你的至福

量子跳跃

我搜索你在山峰与山谷
我追寻你超越一切维度
我查找你在每一个角落与缝隙
我的探测总是不可思议
但无论我目视何处都会发现
我只不过是在绕行一圈又一圈
在每一场雷暴,在每一阵劲风里
我都能听见你无声的故事

无论我身在何处你都会出场
呈现于每一种滋味,每一阵芳香
我以为我落入了迷幻恍惚
在每一记颤抖中我都感觉你的舞
在每一个情景里我都看到你的视线
你就在那里,仿佛是出于偶然

即使如此,我也曾徘徊
哪怕有这一切,我的生命已更改
我所有的怀疑是徒劳的交战
来自痛苦的回忆中所作的决断
唯有现在,靠着松手释放
我才能沐浴你的光芒
无论我在何处漫游或流浪
我都看见你呈现的堂皇
我是演员,置身每一出戏剧
每一段经历中永恒的元素

在每一次交易,每一个事件
你都在那里,如种子一般
如今我知道了,因为我已见过
原本可能发生的可能原本就有过
没有必要如此拼尽全力
因为那张牌就藏在你的袖子里
为了每一笔财富,每一种声名
那王国就在这里等我们来赢
在每一堆火中,每一个炉膛之内
都有一颗火星把新生带给

所有那些歌曲,从未有人歌唱
依旧年轻的心中所有的渴望
超乎所有的听,超乎所有的看
在你的存在之核心里铺展
一片田野,跨越无限的广大
没有疆界的纯粹是神圣的胚芽
只要我们存在哪怕一瞬间
一刹那我们就将会看见
一个世界,那里无人受难与受苦
那里原初之美从未遭玷污
有光芒闪耀的水域,歌唱的天宇
山岭与沟壑中无一人死去

那着魔的花园,那不可思议之地
我们领受神恩之时曾在此嬉戏
在我们内心略微深一点
在那个废料场,那一堆里面
在那愧疚与悲伤的土墩之下
是又一个明天的璀璨光华
如果你仍有需要信守的誓约
何不纵身投入,何不纵身飞跃。

镜子里的那个人

我想要改变世界,于是有一天我起床朝镜子里看。那个人回望并说道:"没有多少时间了。地球遭受着痛苦摧残。孩子们正在挨饿。各个民族仍被不信任与仇恨所分割。每个地方空气和水都已被污染到几乎无可救药的地步。做点什么吧!"

镜子里的那个人感觉非常愤怒与绝望。一切看上去都像是一团糟,一个悲剧,一场灾难。我断定他必然是对的。我对这些事情不也感到恐怖吗,就像他一样?这颗星球正在被耗尽,被抛弃。想象离现在仅仅一代人之后在世上的生活都让我不寒而栗。

不难找到想要解决地球的问题的好人。当我倾听他们的解决方案时,我想到:"有这么多的善意,这么多的关注。"夜里上床之前,镜子里的那个人严肃地向我回望。"现在我们会有进展的,"他宣布,"如果人人都尽自己一份力的话。"

但并非人人都尽自己的一份力。有人做了,但他们能力挽狂澜吗?痛苦、饥馑、仇恨和污染会得到解决吗?光是希望并不能做到这一点——这我知道。当我第二天早晨醒来时,镜子里的那个人神情困惑。"也许没有希望了。"他低声说道。随后一道狡黠的目光出现在他的眼中,他耸了耸肩:"但你我会幸存下来的。至少我们过得挺好。"

他这么说我感觉很奇怪。这儿有什么东西出了很大的错。一丝怀疑掠过我脑际,以前从未变得如此明朗过。如果镜子里

143

的那个人不是我呢？他感觉很隔膜。他看到"外面"有问题要解决。也许它们会得到解决，也许不会。他都能过下去。但我不是这么感觉——那些问题并不在"外面"，其实。我感觉它们在我之内。一个孩子在埃塞俄比亚哭泣，一只海鸥在一场石油泄漏中可怜地挣扎，一只山上的大猩猩被残忍地猎杀，一个少年战士在恐惧中颤抖，当他听见飞机从头顶飞过：这一切难道不正发生在我之内吗，当我耳闻目睹它们的时候？

下一回我朝镜子里看，那个回望的人已开始淡化了。那毕竟只是一个影像而已。它向我呈现了一个被禁锢在皮肤与骨肉的整洁封装里的孤独之人。"我曾经以为你就是我吗？"我开始疑惑起来。我并不那么疏离而又害怕。生命的苦痛触碰到我，但相比之下生命的欢乐是何其强大。而单靠它就可以治愈了。生命是生活的治愈者，我能为地球做到最多的就是做它的爱子。

镜子里的那个人畏畏缩缩，局促不安。他对于爱从未想过那么多。看见"问题"要容易得多，因为爱意味着彻底的自我坦诚。哎呀！

"哦，朋友！"我低声对他说，"你认为有任何东西可以没有爱而解决问题吗？"镜子里的那个人并不确定。独处了那么久，不信任他人也不被他人所信任，它倾向于将自己与生活的现实相分离。"爱比痛苦更真实吗？"他问。

"我不能保证是这样。但可能是的。让我们去发现吧，"我说。我咧嘴一笑碰了一下镜子。"我们不要再独处了。你愿意做我的同伴吗？我听见一支舞蹈要开始了。来吧。"镜子里的那个人害羞地笑了。他渐渐意识到我们可以是最好的朋友。我们可以每天更平和，更有爱，更诚实地对待彼此。

那样就可以改变世界吗？我想会的，因为地球母亲想要我们在照料她的需要时快乐并且爱她。她需要无畏的人站在她这边，他们的勇气来自充当她的一部分，像一个婴儿足够勇敢地学步是因为母亲正伸开她的双臂来接住他一样。当镜子里的那个人对我也对他充满了爱，恐惧就没有地方了。当我们害怕而恐慌时，我们便停止热爱我们的这场生命和这个地球了。我们无所维系。然而任何人又怎能跑去帮助地球，倘若他们感觉无所维系呢？也许地球正在告诉我们她想要什么，而因为不在倾听，我们重又陷入了我们自身的疑惧与恐慌之中。

有一件事我知道：当我是地球的孩子时我从不感觉孤单。我不必执着于我个人的幸存，只要我意识到，日复一日，生命的一切尽在我之内。孩子和他们的苦痛；孩子和他们的欢乐。海洋在太阳之下膨胀；海洋用黑色的石油哭泣。动物在恐惧中被猎杀；动物迸发出活着的纯粹欢乐。

这"世界在我之内"的感觉是我永远想要感到的。镜子里的那个人有时也有他的疑惑。所以我对他很温柔。每天早晨我都碰一下镜子低声说道："哦，朋友，我听见一支舞。你想做我的同伴吗？来吧。"

再看啊，幼海豹

最动人的自然摄影之一是一头幼年毛海豹独自卧在冰上。我肯定你曾经看过——这张图片似乎目不转睛，一只小动物轻信的黑眼睛凝视着照相机，直看到你的心里。当我第一次望着它们时，那对眼睛问道："你会伤害我吗？"我知道回答是会的，因为每年总有数以千计的幼海豹被杀。

很多人被一头幼海豹的无助所触动。他们捐钱来救海豹，于是公众认知开始转变了。当我重新看这幅图片时，这两只分得宽宽的眼睛开始说不一样的话了。现在它们问的是："你了解我吗？"这一回我并未感觉到那么心痛，像我感觉到人类施加于动物的暴力的时候。但我意识到仍有一个巨大的鸿沟在。我对地球上的生命真正了解多少？我对我的小小空间以外的生灵感觉到了什么责任？我如何度过我的生命，才能让活的物质的每一个细胞也都获益？

每个开始困惑于这一切的人都已发现，我想，他们的感觉正从恐惧转向更多亲近作为一个整体的生命。生命的美与神奇开始显得十分个人了；将这颗星球打造为一个花园好让我们所有人在其中生长的可能性已初现曙光。我凝望幼海豹的眼睛，而它们第一次微笑了起来。"谢谢你，"它们说，"你已经给了我希望。"

这就够了吗？希望是一个何等美丽的字眼，但它时常显得极其脆弱。生命仍在遭到无谓的猎杀与毁灭。一头幼海豹独自在冰上或一个幼女在战争中成为孤儿的图像仍以其无助而令人心悸。我意识到没有什么能够最终拯救地球上的生命，除了信任生命本身，信任它治愈的力量，信任它有能力挺过我们的错误并迎接我们回来，在我们学会纠正这些错误的时候。

怀着我心里的这些思绪，我再次望向这张图片。海豹的眼睛此刻似乎更深邃了，而我又在其中看到了我以前漏掉的东西：不可征服的力量。"你并未伤害到我，"它们说，"我不单是一只幼海豹。我就是生命，而生命永远不可能被杀死。它是将我从空间的虚无中产生出来的力量；它在乎我并滋养我的存在对抗一切危险。我是安全的，因为我就是那力量。而你也是。跟我在一起，让我们一同感觉生命的力量，作为同一个生灵在地球之上。"

幼海豹，宽恕我们。再二再三地看看我们吧，看我们在干些什么。那些在你头顶举起棍棒的人们也是父亲和兄弟和儿子。他们也曾爱过，也曾在乎他人。终有一日他们会将那份爱延伸到你身上。千万要确定并且相信。

梦依然继续……

DANCING THE DREAM
POEMS AND REFLECTIONS

MICHAEL JACKSON

INTRODUCTION

When I hear the name Michael Jackson, I think of brilliance, of dazzling stars, lasers and deep emotions. I adore Michael Jackson. I think he is one of the world's biggest and greatest stars, and it just so happens that he is one of the most gifted music makers the world has ever known.

What makes Michael more unique may be the fact that all of his accomplishments, his rewards, have not altered his sensitivity and concern for the welfare of others, or his intense caring and love for his family and friends, and especially all the children the world over.

I think Michael is like litmus paper. He is always trying to learn. He is so intelligent that he is alarmingly bright. He is also very curious and wants to draw from people who have survived. People who have lasted. He is not really of this planet. He is filled with deep emotions that create an unearthly, special, innocent, childlike, wise man that is Michael Jackson. I think Michael appeals to the child in all of us, and I think he has the quality of innocence that we would all like to obtain or to have kept.

He has one of the sharpest wits, he is intelligent and he is cunning – that is a strange word to use about him, because it implies deviousness and he is one of the least devious people I have ever met in my life. He is honesty personified – painfully honest – and vulnerable to the point of pain. He is so giving of himself that, at times, he leaves very little to protect that beautiful inner core that is the essence of him. That is the thing that I love so much about him and that makes the world identify with him in the way it does.

Michael Jackson is, indeed, an international favorite for all ages, an incredible force of incredible energy. In the art of music, he is a pacesetter for quality of production, in the vanguard for high standards of entertainment. What is a genius? What is a living legend? What is a megastar? Michael Jackson–that's all. And just when you think you know him, he gives you more. . .

I think he is one of the finest people to hit this planet, and, in my estimation, he is the true King of Pop, Rock and Soul.

——ELIZABETH TAYLOR

DANCING THE DREAM

Consciousness expresses itself through creation. This world we live in is the dance of the creator. Dancers come and go in the twinkling of an eye but the dance lives on. On many an occasion when I'm dancing, I've felt touched by something sacred. In those moments, I've felt my spirit soar and become one with everything that exists. I become the stars and the moon. I become the lover and the beloved. I become the victor and the vanquished. I become the master and the slave. I become the singer and the song. I become the knower and the known. I keep on dancing and then, it is the eternal dance of creation. The creator and creation merge into one wholeness of joy.

I keep on dancing and dancing……and dancing, until there is only……the dance.

——MICHAEL JACKSON

PLANET EARTH

Planet Earth, my home, my place
A capricious anomaly in the sea of space
Planet Earth, are you just
Floating by, a cloud of dust
A minor globe about to bust
A piece of metal bound to rust
A speck of matter in a mindless void
A lonely spaceship, a large asteroid

Cold as a rock without a hue
Held together with a bit of glue
Something tells me this isn't true
You are my sweetheart, soft and blue
Do you care, have you a part
In the deepest emotions of my own heart
Tender with breezes, caressing and whole
Alive with music, haunting my soul.

In my veins I've felt the mystery
Of corridors of time, books of history
Life songs of ages throbbing in my blood
Have danced the rhythm of the tide and flood
Your misty clouds, your electric storm
Were turbulent tempests in my own form
I've licked the salt, the bitter, the sweet
Of every encounter, of passion, of heat
Your riotous color, your fragrance, your taste
Have thrilled my senses beyond all haste
In your beauty, I've known the how
Of timeless bliss, this moment of now.

Planet Earth, are you just
Floating by, a cloud of dust
A minor globe about to bust
A piece of metal bound to rust
A speck of matter in a mindless void
A lonely spaceship, a large asteroid

Cold as a rock without a hue
Held together with a bit of glue
Something tells me this isn't true
You are my sweetheart, gentle and blue
Do you care, have you a part
In the deepest emotions of my own heart
Tender with breezes, caressing and whole
Alive with music, haunting my soul.

Planet Earth, gentle and blue
With all my heart, I love you.

PART 1

MAGICAL CHILD

Once there was a child and he was free
Deep inside, he felt the laughter
The mirth and play of nature's glee
He was not troubled by thoughts of hereafter
Beauty, love was all he'd see

He knew his power was the power of God
He was so sure, they considered him odd
This power of innocence, of compassion, of light
Threatened the priests and created a fright
In endless ways they sought to dismantle
This mysterious force which they could not handle

In endless ways they tried to destroy
His simple trust, his boundless joy
His invincible armor was a shield of bliss

Nothing could touch it, no venom, no hiss

The child remained in a state of grace
He wasn't confined in time or place
In Technicolor dreams, he frolicked and played
While acting his part, in Eternity he stayed

Soothsayers came and fortunes were told
Some were vehement, others were bold
In denouncing this child, this perplexing creature
With the rest of the world he shared no feature
Is he real? He is so strange
His unpredictable nature knows no range
He puzzles us so, is he straight?
What's his destiny? What's his fate?

And while they whispered and conspired
Through endless rumors to get him tired
To kill his wonder, trample him near
Burn his courage, fuel his fear
The child remained just simple, sincere

All he wanted was the mountain high
Color the clouds, paint the sky
Beyond these boundaries, he wanted to fly
In nature's scheme, never to die

Don't stop this child, he's the father of man
Don't cross his way, he's part of the plan
I am that Child, but so are you
You've just forgotten, just lost the clue

Inside your heart sits a Seer
Between his thoughts, he can hear
A melody simple but wondrously clear
The music of life, so precious, so dear

If you could for one moment know
This spark of creation, this exquisite glow
You would come and dance with me
Kindle this fire so we could see
All the children of the Earth
Weave their magic and give new birth
To a world of freedom with no pain
A world of joy, much more sane

Deep inside, you know it's true
Just find that child, it's hiding in you.

WINGS WITHOUT ME

It was August, and I was looking up at the sky. With one hand shielding my eyes, I made out a falcon soaring on the currents of hot swirling air. Higher and higher it spiraled, until with one unearthly shriek, it disappeared.

All at once I felt left behind. "Why did you grow wings without me?" I mourned. Then my spirit said, "The falcon's way is not the only way. Your thoughts are as free as any bird." So I shut my eyes and my spirit took off, spiraling as high as the falcon and then beyond, so that I was looking down over the whole earth. But something was wrong. Why did I feel so cold and alone?

"You grew wings without me," my heart said. "What good is freedom without love?" So I went quietly to the bed of a sick child and sang him a lullaby. He fell asleep smiling, and my heart took off, joining my spirit as it circled over the earth. I was free and loving, but still something was wrong.

"You grew wings without me," my body said. "Your flights are only imagination." So I looked into books that I had ignored before and read about saints in every age who actually flew. In India, Persia, China, and Spain (even in Los Angeles!), the power of spirit has reached, not just into the heart, but into every cell of the body. "As if carried aloft by a great eagle," Saint Teresa said, "my ecstasy lifted me into the air."

I began to believe in this amazing feat, and for the first time, I didn't feel left behind. I was the falcon and the child and the saint. In my eyes their lives became sacred, and the truth came home: When all life is seen as divine, everyone grows wings.

DANCE OF LIFE

I cannot escape the moon. Its soft beams push aside the curtains at night. I don't even have to see it – a cool blue energy falls across my bed and I am up. I race down the dark hall and swing open the door, not to leave home but to go back to it. "Moon, I'm here!" I shout.

"Good," she replies. "Now give us a little dance."

But my body has started moving long before she says anything. When did it start? I can't remember – my body has always been moving. Since childhood I have reacted to the moon this way, as her favorite lunatic, and not just hers. The stars draw me near, close enough so that I see through their twinkling act. They're dancing, too, doing a soft molecular jiggle that makes my carbon atoms jump in time.

With my arms flung wide, I head for the sea, which brings out another dance in me. Moon dancing is slow inside, and soft as blue shadows on the lawn. When the surf booms, I hear the heart of the earth, and the tempo picks up. I feel the dolphins leaping in the white foam, trying to fly, and almost flying when the waves curl high to the heavens. Their tails leave arcs of light as plankton glow in the waves. A school of minnows rises up, flashing silver in the moonlight like a new constellation.

"Ah!" the sea says. "Now we're gathering a crowd."

I run along the beach, catching waves with one foot and dodging them with the other. I hear faint popping sounds – a hundred panicky sand crabs are ducking into their holes, just in case. But I'm racing now, sometimes on my toes, sometimes running flat-out.

I throw my head back and a swirling nebula says, "Fast now, twirl!"

Grinning, ducking my head for balance, I start to spin as wildly as I can. This is my favorite dance, because it contains a secret. The faster I twirl, the more I am still inside. My dance is all motion without, all silence within. As much as I love to make music, it's the unheard music that never dies. And silence is my real dance, though it never moves. It stands aside, my choreographer of grace, and blesses each finger and toe.

I have forgotten the moon now and the sea and the dolphins, but I am in their joy more than ever. As far away as a star, as near as a grain of sand, the presence rises, shimmering with light. I could be in it forever, it is so loving and warm. But touch it once, and light shoots forth from the stillness. It quivers and thrills me, and I know my fate is to show others that this silence, this light, this blessing is my dance. I take this gift only to give it again.

"Quick, give!" says the light.

As never before, I try to obey, inventing new steps, new gestures of joy. All at once I sense where I am, running back up the hill. The light in my bedroom is on. Seeing it brings me back down. I begin to feel my pounding heart, the drowsiness in my arms, the warm blood in my legs. My cells want to dance slower. "Can we walk a little?" they ask. "It's been kind of wild."

"Sure." I laugh, slowing to an easy amble.

I turn the doorknob, panting lightly, glad to be tired. Crawling back into bed, I remember something that I always wonder at. They say that some of the stars that we see overhead aren't really there. Their light takes millions of years to reach us, and all we are doing is looking into the past, into a bygone moment when those stars could still shine.

"So what does a star do after it quits shining?" I ask myself. "Maybe it dies."

"Oh, no," a voice in my head says. "A star can never die. It just turns into a smile and melts back into the cosmic music, the dance of life." I like that thought, the last one I have before my eyes close. With a smile, I melt back into the music myself.

WHEN BABIES SMILE

When dreamers dream and kiss their lover
And rainbows weave and splash their color
Those are moments so gloriously alive
We take the plunge, take the dive
Into the abyss
We are suspended awhile
Those are moments when babies smile.

Those are moments when fate is unsealed
Nothing is impossible and we are healed
We can soar, we can fly
Walk on fire, navigate the sky
In the light of a glittering star
There's no distance, nothing is far
Those are moments of innocent guile
In the glow
We are suspended awhile
Those are moments when babies smile.

Those are moments when the heart is tender
When seascapes gleam in magnificent splendor
When the laughter of Heaven reverberates the Earth
And we are renewed in a new birth
In a timeless Eternity
In the angels' fraternity
We romp and roll
The playground of our soul
In the twilight
We are suspended awhile
Those are moments when babies smile.

Those are moments we're one with God
All is well, nothing is odd
In silent reflection
We feel our perfection
We are the source, we are the crucible
Nothing can hurt us, for we are invincible
There is no sin, there is no sinner
We can only win, we have felt the glimmer
In the bliss
We're floating awhile

Those are moments when babies smile.

Kingdoms topple, lose their class
Civilizations crumble, ages pass
Turbulent tempests ravage the seas
Violent killings, despite our pleas
But dewdrops sparkle when children play
Tyrants cry, there's nothing to slay
Fairies dance and goblins sing
All are crowned, all are king
In the Garden
We frolic awhile
Those are moments when babies smile.

BUT THE HEART SAID NO

They saw the poor living in cardboard shacks, so they knocked the shacks down and built projects. Huge blocks of cement and glass towered over asphalt parking lots. Somehow it wasn't much like home, even home in a shack. "What do you expect?" they asked impatiently. "You're too poor to live like us. Until you can do better for yourselves, you should be grateful, shouldn't you?"

The head said yes, but the heart said no.

They needed more electricity in the city, so they found a mountain stream to dam. As the waters rose, dead rabbits and deer floated by; baby birds too young to fly drowned in the nest while mother birds cried helplessly. "It's not a pretty sight," they said, "but now a million people can run their air conditioners all summer. That's more important than one mountain stream, isn't it?"

The head said yes, but the heart said no.

They saw oppression and terrorism in a far-off land, so they made war against it. Bombs reduced the country to rubble. Its population cowered in fear, and every day more villagers were buried in rough wooden coffins. "You have to be prepared to make sacrifices," they said. "If some innocent bystanders get hurt, isn't that just the price one must pay for peace?"

The head said yes, but the heart said no.

The years rolled by and they got old. Sitting in their comfortable houses, they took stock. "We've had a good life," they said, "and we did the right thing." Their children looked down and asked why poverty, pollution, and war were still unsolved. "You'll find out soon enough," they replied. "Human beings are weak and selfish. Despite our best efforts, these problems will never really end."

The head said yes, but the children looked into their hearts and whispered, "No!"

CHILDREN OF THE WORLD

Children of the world, we'll do it
We'll meet on endless shores
Making sandcastles and floating our boats
While people fight and defend their point of view
Forever putting on masks that are new
We'll swing the tide of time and do it.

Children of the world, we'll do it
With song and dance and innocent bliss
And the soft caress of a loving kiss
We'll do it.

While traders trade and haggle their price
And politicians try so hard to be nice
We'll meet on endless shores and floating our boats
We'll do it.

While lawyers argue and doctors treat
Stockbrokers quote the price on meat
While preachers preach and ring the bell
Carpetbaggers with something to sell
We'll sing and dance in innocent bliss
With the soft caress of a loving kiss
We'll do it
Meeting on endless shores
Making sandcastles and floating our boats
We'll do it.

We'll ride a rainbow, a cloud, a storm
Flying in the wind, we'll change our form
We'll touch the stars, embrace the moon
We'll break the barrier and be there soon

While architects plan their buildings high
And trade unions raise their hue and cry
While boardroom squabbles generate heat
And in secret places dealers meet
We'll sing and dance in innocent bliss
With the soft caress of a loving kiss
We'll do it.

While philosophers grapple and continue to tackle
Endless dilemmas of body and mind
Physicists wander, continue to ponder
Perennial questions of space and time
Archaeologists survey, continue to dig
Bygone treasures small and big

Psychologists probe, analyze the tears
Of hysterical notions, phobias, fears

While priests take confession
In a serious session
And people struggle
In the hustle and bustle
In the noise and din
On the meaning of sin
We'll touch the stars, embrace the moon
Break the barrier, arrive there soon
Ride the rainbow, the cloud, the storm
Flying in the wind, changing our form

Children of the world, we'll do it
With song and dance and innocent bliss
The soft caress of a loving kiss
We'll do it.

SO THE ELEPHANTS MARCH

A curious fact about elephants is this: In order to survive, they mustn't fall down. Every other animal can stumble and get back up again. But an elephant always stands up, even to sleep. If one of the herd slips and falls, it is helpless. It lies on its side, a prisoner of its own weight. Although the other elephants will press close around it in distress and try to lift it up again, there isn't usually much they can do. With slow heaving breaths, the fallen elephant dies. The others stand vigil, then slowly move on.

This is what I learned from nature books, but I wonder if they are right. Isn't there another reason why elephants can't fall down? Perhaps they have decided not to. Not to fall down is their mission. As the wisest and most patient of animals, they made a pact – I imagine it was eons ago, when the ice ages were ending. Moving in great herds across the face of the earth, the elephants first spied tiny men prowling the tall grasses with their flint spears.

"What fear and anger this creature has," the elephants thought. "But he is going to inherit the earth. We are wise enough to see that. Let us set an example for him."

Then the elephants put their grizzled heads together and pondered. What kind of example could they show to man? They could show him that their power was much greater than his, for that was certainly true. They could display their anger before him, which was terrible enough to uproot whole forests. Or they could lord it over man through fear, trampling his fields and crushing his huts.

In moments of great frustration, wild elephants will do all of these things, but as a group, putting their heads together, they decided that man would learn best from a kinder message.

"Let us show him our reverence for life," they said. And from that day on, elephants have been silent, patient, peaceful creatures. They let men ride them and harness them like slaves. They permit children to laugh at their tricks in the circus, exiled from the great African plains where they once lived as lords.

But the elephants' most important message is in their movement. For they know that to live is to move. Dawn after dawn, age after age, the herds march on, one great mass of life that never falls down, an unstoppable force of peace.

Innocent animals, they do not suspect that after all this time, they will fall from a bullet by the thousands. They will lie in the dust, mutilated by our shameless greed. The great males fall first, so that their tusks can be made into trinkets. Then the females fall, so that men may have trophies. The babies run screaming from the smell of their own mothers' blood, but it does them no good to run from the guns. Silently, with no one to nurse them, they will die, too, and all their bones bleach in the sun.

In the midst of so much death, the elephants could just give up. All they have to do is drop to the ground. That is enough. They don't need a bullet: Nature has given them the dignity to lie down and find their rest. But they remember their ancient pact and their pledge to us, which is sacred.

So the elephants march on, and every tread beats out words in the dust: "Watch, learn, love. Watch, learn, love." Can you hear them? One day in shame, the ghosts of ten thousand lords of the plains will say, "We do not hate you. Don't you see at last? We were willing to fall, so that you, dear small ones, will never fall again."

THE BOY AND THE PILLOW

A wise father wanted to teach his young son a lesson. "Here is a pillow covered in silk brocade and stuffed with the rarest goose down in the land," he said. "Go to town and see what it will fetch."

First the boy went to the marketplace, where he saw a wealthy feather merchant. "What will you give me for this pillow?" he asked. The merchant narrowed his eyes. "I will give you fifty gold ducats, for I see that this is a rare treasure indeed."

The boy thanked him and went on. Next he saw a farmer's wife peddling vegetables by the side of the road. "What will you give me for this pillow?" he asked. She felt it and exclaimed, "How soft it is! I'll give you one piece of silver, for I long to lay my weary head on such a pillow."

The boy thanked her and walked on. Finally he saw a young peasant girl washing the steps of a church. "What will you give me for this pillow?" he asked. Looking at him with a strange smile, she replied, "I'll give you a penny, for I can see that your pillow is hard compared to these stones." Without hesitation, the boy laid the pillow at her feet.

When he got home, he said to his father, "I have gotten the best price for your pillow." And he held out the penny.

"What?" his father exclaimed. "That pillow was worth a hundred gold ducats at least."

"That's what a wealthy merchant saw," the boy said, "but being greedy, he offered me fifty. I got a better offer than that. A farmer's wife offered me one piece of silver."

"Are you mad?" his father said. "When is one piece of silver worth more than fifty gold ducats?"

"When it's offered out of love," the boy replied. "If she had given me more, she wouldn't have been able to feed her children. Yet I got a better offer than that. I saw a peasant girl washing the steps of a church who offered me this penny."

"You have lost your wits completely," his father said, shaking his head. "When is a penny worth more than a piece of silver?"

"When it's offered out of devotion," the boy replied. "For she was laboring for her Lord, and the steps of His house seemed softer than any pillow. Poorer than the poorest, she still had time for God. And that is why I offered her the pillow."

At this the wise father smiled and embraced his son, and with a tear in his eye he murmured, "You have learned well."

ENOUGH FOR TODAY

Dance rehearsals can go on past midnight, but this time I stopped at ten. "I hope you don't mind," I said, looking up into space, "but that's enough for today."

A voice from the control room spoke. "You okay?"

"A little tired, I guess," I said.

I slipped on a windbreaker and headed down the hall. Running footsteps came up behind me. I was pretty sure who they belonged to. "I know you too well," she said, catching up with me. "What's really wrong?"

I hesitated. "Well, I don't know how this sounds, but I saw a picture today in the papers. A dolphin had drowned in a fishing net. From the way its body was tangled in the lines, you could read so much agony. Its eyes were vacant, yet there was still that smile, the one dolphins never lose, even when they die..." My voice trailed off.

She put her hand lightly in mine. "I know, I know."

"No, you don't know all of it yet. It's not just that

I felt sad, or had to face the fact that an innocent being had died. Dolphins love to dance – of all the creatures in the sea, that's their mark. Asking nothing from us, they cavort in the waves while we marvel. They race ahead of ships, not to get there first but to tell us, 'It's all meant to be play. Keep to your course, but dance while you do it.'

"So there I was, in the middle of rehearsal, and I thought, 'They're killing a dance.' And then it seemed only right to stop. I can't keep the dance from being killed, but at least I can pause in memory, as one dancer to another. Does that make any sense?"

Her eyes were tender. "Sure, in its way. Probably we'll wait years before everyone agrees on how to solve this thing. So many interests are involved. But it's too frustrating waiting for improvements tomorrow. Your heart wanted to have its say now."

"Yes," I said, pushing the door open for her. "I just had this feeling, and that's enough for today."

MARK OF THE ANCIENTS

He had lived in the desert all his life, but for me it was all new. "See that footprint in the sand?" he asked, pointing to a spot by the cliff. I looked as close as I could. "No, I don't see anything."

"That's just the point." He laughed. "Where you can't see a print, that's where the Ancient Ones walked."

We went on a little farther, and he pointed to an opening, high up on the sandstone wall. "See that house up there?" he asked. I squinted hard. "There's nothing to see."

"You're a good student." He smiled. "Where there's no roof or chimney, that's where the Ancient Ones are most likely to have lived."

We rounded a bend, and before us was spread a fabulous sight – thousands upon thousands of desert flowers in bloom. "Can you see any missing?" he asked me. I shook my head. "It's just wave after wave of loveliness."

"Yes," he said in a low voice. "Where nothing is missing, that's where the Ancient Ones harvested the most."

I thought about all this, about how generations had once lived in harmony with the earth, leaving no marks to scar the places they inhabited. At camp that night I said, "You left out one thing."

"What's that?" he asked.

"Where are the Ancient Ones buried?"

Without reply, he poked his stick into the fire. A bright flame shot up, licked the air, and disappeared. My teacher gave me a glance to ask if I understood this lesson. I sat very still, and my silence told him I did.

HEAL THE WORLD

There's a place in your heart
And I know that it is love
And this place could be much brighter
Than tomorrow
And if you really try
You'll find there's no need to cry
In this place I feel there's no hurt or sorrow

There are ways to get there

If you care enough for the living
Make a little space
Make a better place
Heal the world
Make it a better place
For you and for me
And the entire human race

There are people dying
If you care enough for the living
Make a better place
For you and for me

If you want to know why, there's a love that cannot lie
Love is strong, it cares for only joyful giving
If we try, we shall see
In this bliss we cannot feel
Fear or dread

Then we just stop existing and start living
Then it feels that always
Love's enough for us growing
Make a better world
Make a better world
Heal the world
Make it a better place
For you and for me
And the entire human race

There are people dying
If you care enough for the living
Make a better place for you and for me

And the dream we were conceived in
Will reveal its joyful face
And the world we once believed in

Will shine again in grace

Then why do we keep strangling life
Wound this Earth, crucify its soul
Tho it's plain to see
This world is heavenly
We could be God's glow
We could fly so high
Let our spirit never die

In my heart I feel you are all my brothers
Create a world with no fear
Together we'll cry happy tears
So that nations turn their swords into plowshares
We could really get there
If you cared enough for the living
Make a little space
To make a better place
Heal the world
Make it a better place
For you and for me
And the entire human race

There are people dying
If you care enough for the living
Make a better place
For you and for me
Heal the world
Make it a better place
For you and for me
And the entire human race

There are people dying
If you care enough for the living
Make a better place
For you and for me

Heal the world
Make it a better place
For you and for me
And the entire human race

There are people dying
If you care enough for the living
Make a better place
For you and for me

There are people dying
If you care enough for the living
Make a better place
For you and for me

There are people dying
If you care enough for the living
Make a better place
For you and for me
For you and for me
For you and for me
For you and for me
For you and for me
You and for me
You and for me

CHILDREN

Children show me in their playful smiles the divine in everyone. This simple goodness shines straight from their hearts. This has so much to teach. If a child wants chocolate ice cream, he just asks for it. Adults get tangled up in complications over whether to eat the ice cream or not. A child simply enjoys.

What we need to learn from children isn't childish. Being with them connects us to the deep wisdom of life, which is everpresent and only asks to be lived. Now, when the world is so confused and its problems so complicated, I feel we need our children more than ever. Their natural wisdom points the way to solutions that lie, waiting to be recognized, within our own hearts.

MOTHER

Eons of time I've been gestating
To take a form been hesitating
From the unmanifest this cosmic conception
On this earth a fantastic reception
And then one fateful August morn
From your being I was born
With tender love you nurtured a seed
To your own distress you paid no heed
Unmindful of any risk and danger
You decided upon this lonely stranger

Rainbows, clouds, the deep blue sky
Glittering birds that fly on high
Out of fragments you've made my whole
From the elements you fashioned my soul
Mother dear, you gave me life
Because of you, no struggle or strife
You gave me joy and position
Cared for me without condition
And if I ever change this world
It's from the emotions you've unfurl'd
Your compassion is so sweet and dear
Your finest feelings I can hear
I can sense your faintest notion
The wondrous magic of your love potion

And now that I have come so far
Met with every king and czar
Encountered every color and creed
Of every passion, every greed
I go back to that starry night
With not a fear for muscle or might
You taught me how to stand and fight
For every single wrong and right
Every day without a hold
I will treasure what you've mold
I will remember every kiss
Your sweet words I'll never miss
No matter where I go from here
You're in my heart, my mother dear.

MAGIC

My idea of magic doesn't have much to do with stage tricks and illusions. The whole world abounds in magic. When a whale plunges out of the sea like a newborn mountain, you gasp in unexpected delight. What magic! But a toddler who sees his first tadpole flashing in a mud puddle feels the same thrill. Wonder fills his heart, because he has glimpsed for an instant the playfulness of life.

When I see the clouds whisked away from a snow-capped peak, I feel like shouting, "Bravo!" Nature, the best of all magicians, has delivered another thrill. She has exposed the real illusion, our inability to be amazed by her wonders. Every time the sun rises, Nature is repeating one command: "Behold!" Her magic is infinitely lavish, and in return all we have to do is appreciate it.

What delight Nature must feel when she makes stars out of swirling gas and empty space. She flings them like spangles from a velvet cape, a billion reasons for us to awaken in pure joy. When we open our hearts and appreciate all she has given us, Nature finds her reward. The sound of applause rolls across the universe, and she bows.

THE FISH THAT WAS THIRSTY

One night a baby fish was sleeping under some coral when God appeared to him in a dream. "I want you to go forth with a message to all the fish in the sea," God said.

"What should I tell them?" the little fish asked.

"Just tell them you're thirsty," God replied. "And see what they do." Then without another word, He disappeared.

The next morning the little fish woke up and remembered his dream. "What a strange thing God wants me to do," he thought to himself. But as soon as he saw a large tuna swimming by, the little fish piped up, "Excuse me, but I'm thirsty."

"Then you must be a fool," the tuna said. And with a disdainful flick of his tail, he swam away.

The little fish did feel rather foolish, but he had his orders. The next fish he saw was a grinning shark. Keeping a safe distance, the little fish called out, "Excuse me, sir, but I'm thirsty."

"Then you must be crazy," the shark replied. Noticing a rather hungry look in the shark's eye, the little fish swam away quickly.

All day he met cod and mackerels and swordfish and groupers, but every time he made his short speech, they turned their backs and would have nothing to do with him. Feeling hopelessly confused, the little fish sought out the wisest creature in the sea, who happened to be an old blue whale with three harpoon scars on his side.

"Excuse me, but I'm thirsty!" the little fish shouted, wondering if the old whale could even see him, he was such a tiny speck. But the wise one stopped in his tracks. "You've seen God, haven't you?" he said.

"How did you know?"

"Because I was thirsty once, too." The old whale laughed.

The little fish looked very surprised. "Please tell me what this message from God means," he implored.

"It means that we are looking for Him in the wrong places," the old whale explained. "We look high and low for God, but somehow He's not there. So we blame Him and tell ourselves that He must have forgotten us. Or else we decide that He left a long time ago, if He was ever around."

"How strange," the little fish said, "to miss what is everywhere."

"Very strange," the old whale agreed. "Doesn't it remind you of fish who say they're thirsty?"

INNOCENCE

It's easy to mistake being innocent for being simpleminded or naive. We all want to seem sophisticated; we all want to seem street-smart. To be innocent is to be "out of it."

Yet there is a deep truth in innocence. A baby looks in his mother's eyes, and all he sees is love. As innocence fades away, more complicated things take its place. We think we need to outwit others and scheme to get what we want. We begin to spend a lot of energy protecting ourselves. Then life turns into a struggle. People have no choice but to be street-smart. How else can they survive?

When you get right down to it, survival means seeing things the way they really are and responding. It means being open. And that's what innocence is. It's simple and trusting like a child, not judgmental and committed to one narrow point of view. If you are locked into a pattern of thinking and responding, your creativity gets blocked. You miss the freshness and magic of the moment. Learn to be innocent again, and that freshness never fades.

TRUST

As I was feeding squirrels in the park, I noticed a small one that didn't seem to trust me. While the others came close enough to eat out of my hand, he kept his distance. I threw a peanut his way. He edged up, grabbed it nervously, and ran off. Next time he must have felt less afraid, because he came a little closer. The safer he felt, the more he trusted me. Finally he sat right at my feet, as bold as any squirrel clamoring for the next peanut.

Trust is like that–it always seems to come down to trusting in yourself. Others can't overcome fear for you; you have to do it on your own. It's hard, because fear and doubt hold on tight. We are afraid of being rejected, of being hurt once more. So we keep a safe distance. We think separating ourselves from others will protect us, but that doesn't work, either. It leaves us feeling alone and unloved.

Trusting yourself begins by recognizing that it's okay to be afraid. Having fear is not the problem, because everyone feels anxious and insecure sometimes. The problem is not being honest enough to admit your fear. Whenever I accept my own doubt and insecurity, I'm more open to other people. The deeper I go into myself, the stronger I become, because I realize that my real self is much bigger than any fear.

In accepting yourself completely, trust becomes complete. There is no longer any separation between people, because there is no longer any separation inside. In the space where fear used to live, love is allowed to grow.

COURAGE

It's curious what takes courage and what doesn't. When I step out on stage in front of thousands of people, I don't feel that I'm being brave. It can take much more courage to express true feelings to one person. When I think of courage, I think of the Cowardly Lion in *The Wizard of Oz*. He was always running away from danger. He often cried and shook with fear. But he was also sharing his real feelings with those he loved, even though he didn't always like those feelings.

That takes real courage, the courage to be intimate. Expressing your feelings is not the same as falling apart in front of someone else – it's being accepting and true to your heart, whatever it may say. When you have the courage to be intimate, you know who you are, and you're willing to let others see that. It's scary, because you feel so vulnerable, so open to rejection. But without self-acceptance, the other kind of courage, the kind heroes show in movies, seems hollow. In spite of the risks, the courage to be honest and intimate opens the way to self-discovery. It offers what we all want, the promise of love.

LOVE

Love is a funny thing to describe. It's so easy to feel and yet so slippery to talk about. It's like a bar of soap in the bathtub–you have it in your hand until you hold on too tight.

Some people spend their lives looking for love outside themselves. They think they have to grasp it in order to have it. But love slips away like that wet bar of soap.

Holding on to love is not wrong, but you need to learn to hold it lightly, caressingly. Let it fly when it wants. When it's allowed to be free, love is what makes life alive, joyful, and new. It's the juice and energy that motivates my music, my dancing, everything. As long as love is in my heart, it's everywhere.

GOD

It's strange that God doesn't mind expressing Himself/Herself in all the religions of the world, while people still cling to the notion that their way is the only right way. Whatever you try to say about God, someone will take offense, even if you say everyone's love of God is right for them.

For me the form God takes is not the most important thing. What's most important is the essence. My songs and dances are outlines for Him to come in and fill. I hold out the form, She puts in the sweetness.

I've looked up at the night sky and beheld the stars so intimately close, it was as if my grandmother had made them for me. "How rich, how sumptuous," I thought. In that moment I saw God in His creation. I could as easily have seen Her in the beauty of a rainbow, the grace of a deer bounding through a meadow, the truth of a father's kiss. But for me the sweetest contact with God has no form. I close my eyes, look within, and enter a deep soft silence. The infinity of God's creation embraces me. We are one.

HOW I MAKE MUSIC

People ask me how I make music. I tell them I just step into it. It's like stepping into a river and joining the flow. Every moment in the river has its song. So I stay in the moment and listen.

What I hear is never the same. A walk through the woods brings a light, crackling song: Leaves rustle in the wind, birds chatter and squirrels scold, twigs crunch underfoot, and the beat of my heart holds it all together. When you join the flow, the music is inside and outside, and both are the same. As long as I can listen to the moment, I'll always have music.

RYAN WHITE

Ryan White, symbol of justice
Or child of innocence, messenger of love
Where are you now, where have you gone?

Ryan White, I miss your sunny days
We carelessly frolicked in extended plays

I miss you, Ryan White
I miss your smile, innocent and bright
I miss your glory, I miss your light

Ryan White, symbol of contradiction
Child of Irony, or child of fiction?

I think of your shattered life
Of your struggle, of your strife

While ladies dance in the moonlit night
Champagne parties on chartered cruises
I see your wasted form, your ghostly sight
I feel your festering wounds, your battered bruises

Ryan White, symbol of agony and pain
Of ignorant fear gone insane
In a hysterical society
With free-floating anxiety
And feigned piety

I miss you, Ryan White
You showed us how to stand and fight
In the rain you were a cloudburst of joy
The sparkle of hope in every girl and boy

In the depths of your anguished sorrow
Was the dream of another tomorrow.

THE ELUSIVE SHADOW

Even tho I traveled far
The door to my soul stayed ajar

In the agony of mortal fear
Your music I did not hear
Thru twisting roads in memory lane
I bore my cross in pain

It was a journey of madness
Of anguish born in sadness
I wandered high and low
Recoiled from every blow
Looking for that stolen nectar
In my heart that long-lost scepter
In all those haunted faces
I searched for my oasis

In a way it was in a drunken craze
A cruel hysteria, a blurry haze
Many a time I tried to break
This shadow following me I could not shake
Many a time in the noisy crowd
In the hustle and bustle of the din so loud
I peered behind to see its trace
I could not lose it in any place

It was only when I broke all ties
After the stillness of the shrieking cries
In the depths of those heaving sighs
The imagined sorrow of a thousand lies
I suddenly stared in your fiery eyes
All at once I found my goal
The elusive shadow was my soul.

ON CHILDREN OF THE WORLD

We have to heal our wounded world. The chaos, despair, and senseless destruction we see today are a result of the alienation that people feel from each other and their environment. Often this alienation has its roots in an emotionally deprived childhood. Children have had their childhood stolen from them. A child's mind needs the nourishment of mystery, magic, wonder, and excitement. I want my work to help people rediscover the child that's hiding in them.

TWO BIRDS

It's hard to tell them what I feel for you. They haven't ever met you, and no one has your picture. So how can they ever understand your mystery? Let's give them a clue:

Two birds sit in a tree. One eats cherries, while the other looks on. Two birds fly through the air. One's song drops like crystal from the sky while the other keeps silent. Two birds wheel in the sun. One catches the light on its silver feathers, while the other spreads wings of invisibility.

It's easy to guess which bird I am, but they'll never find you. Unless...

Unless they already know a love that never interferes, that watches from beyond, that breathes free in the invisible air. Sweet bird, my soul, your silence is so precious. How long will it be before the world hears your song in mine?

Oh, that is a day I hunger for!

THE LAST TEAR

Your words stabbed my heart, and I cried tears of pain. "Get out!" I shouted. "These are the last tears I'll ever cry for you." So you left.

I waited hours, but you didn't return. That night by myself I cried tears of frustration.

I waited weeks, but you had nothing to say. Thinking of your voice, I cried tears of loneliness.

I waited months, but you left no sign for me. In the depths of my heart, I cried tears of despair.

How strange that all these tears could not wash away the hurt! Then one thought of love pierced my bitterness. I remembered you in the sunlight, with a smile as sweet as May wine. A tear of gratitude started to fall, and miraculously, you were back. Soft fingers touched my cheek, and you bent over for a kiss.

"Why have you come?" I whispered.

"To wipe away your last tear," you replied. "It was the one you saved for me."

ECSTASY

I was born to never die
To live in bliss, to never cry
To speak the truth and never lie
To share my love without a sigh
To stretch my arms without a tie
This is my dance, this is my high
It's not a secret, can't you see
Why can't we all live in ecstasy

Ecstasy   Ecstasy
Why can't we all
Live in Ecstasy.

Without a guilt, without regret

I am here to forget
Tainted memories of imagined sin
In every friend, kith and kin

We have come to celebrate here
The getting rid of every fear
Of every notion, every seed
Of any separation, caste, or creed.

This alienation, fragmentation, abomination
Of separation, exploitation, isolation
This cruelty, hysteria, absolute madness
This anger, anxiety, overflowing sadness
Disrupted ecology, wanton destruction
Diseased biology, nature's obstruction
Endangered species, environmental pollution
Holes in the ozone, defying solution
Is not knowing the spark that lights my interior
Is the same fire, glowing in every man, child, and mother superior

We have come to celebrate here
The getting rid of every fear
Of every notion, every seed
Of any separation, caste, or creed.

Feeling free, let us fly
Into the boundless, beyond the sky
For we were born to never die
To live in bliss, to never cry
To speak the truth and never lie
To share our love without a sigh
To stretch our arms without a tie

This is our dance, this is our high
It's not a secret, can't you see
Why can't we all live in ecstasy

Ecstasy   Ecstasy
Why can't we all
Live in Ecstasy.

BERLIN 1989

They hated the Wall, but what could they do? It was too strong to break through.

They feared the Wall, but didn't that make sense? Many who tried to climb over it were killed.

They distrusted the Wall, but who wouldn't? Their enemies refused to tear down one brick, no matter how long the peace talks dragged on.

The Wall laughed grimly. "I'm teaching you a good lesson," it boasted. "If you want to build for eternity, don't bother with stones. Hatred, fear, and distrust are so much stronger."

They knew the Wall was right, and they almost gave up. Only one thing stopped them. They remembered who was on the other side. Grandmother, cousin, sister, wife. Beloved faces that yearned to be seen.

"What's happening?" the Wall asked, trembling. Without knowing what they did, they were looking through the Wall, trying to find their dear ones. Silently, from one person to another, love kept up its invisible work.

"Stop it!" the Wall shrieked. "I'm falling apart." But it was too late. A million hearts had found each other. The Wall had fallen before it came down.

MOTHER EARTH

I was walking along the beach one winter day. Looking down, I saw a wave push a feather up on the sand. It was a sea gull feather stained with oil. I picked it up and felt the dark slick film on my fingers. I couldn't help wondering if the bird had survived. Was it all right out there? I knew it wasn't.

I felt sad to think how carelessly we treat our home. The earth we all share is not just a rock tossed through space but a living, nurturing being. She cares for us; she deserves our care in return. We've been treating Mother Earth the way some people treat a rental apartment. Just trash it and move on.

But there's no place to move on to now. We have brought our garbage and our wars and our racism to every part of the world. We must begin to clean her up, and that means cleaning up our own hearts and minds first, because they led us to poison our dear planet. The sooner we change, the easier it will be to feel our love for Mother Earth and the love she so freely gives back to us.

WISE LITTLE GIRL

I know a wise little girl who cannot walk. She is confined to a wheelchair, and she may spend the rest of her life there, since her doctors hold out almost no hope of ever making her paralyzed legs better.

When I first met this little girl, she flashed me a smile that burned me with its blazing happiness. How open she was! She wasn't hiding out from self-pity or asking for approval or protecting herself from a sense of shame. She felt completely innocent about not being able to walk, like a puppy that has no idea if it is a mongrel or champion of the breed.

She made no judgments about herself. That was her wisdom.

I have seen the same wise look in other children, "poor" children as society sees them, because they lack food, money, secure homes, or healthy bodies. By the time they reach a certain age, many of these children grasp just how bad their situation is. The way that adults look at their lives robs them of that first innocence that is so precious and rare. They begin to believe that they should feel bad about themselves; that this is "right."

But this wise little girl, being only four, floated above pity and shame like a carefree sparrow. She took my heart in her hands and made it as weightless as a cotton puff, so that it was impossible for me to even begin to think, "What a terrible thing." All I saw was light and love. In their innocence, very young children know themselves to be light and love. If we will allow them, they can teach us to see ourselves the same way.

One sparkle from a little girl's gaze contains the same knowledge that Nature implants at the heart of every life-form. It is life's silent secret, not to be put into words. It just knows. It knows peace and how not to hurt. It knows that even the least breath is a gesture of gratitude to the Creator. It smiles to be alive, waiting patiently for ages of ignorance and sorrow to pass away like a mirage.

I see this knowledge showing itself in the eyes of children more and more, which makes me think that their innocence is growing stronger. They are going to disarm us adults, and that will be enough to disarm the world. They feel no reason to spoil the environment, and so the environment will be cleaned up without a quarrel. A wise little girl told me the future when she looked at me, so full of peace and contentment. I rejoice in trusting her above all the experts. As light and love drive away our guilt and shame, her prophecy must come true.

I YOU WE

I said you had to do it. You said you didn't want to. We talked about it, and we agreed that maybe I could help.

I said you were wrong. You insisted you were right. We held each other's hand, and right and wrong disappeared.

I began crying. You began crying, too. We embraced, and between us grew a flower of peace.

How I love this mystery called We! Where does it come from, out of thin air? I thought about this mystery, and I realized something: We must be love's favorite child, because until I reach out for you, We is not even there. It arrives on the wings of tenderness; it speaks through our silent understanding. When I laugh at myself, it smiles. When I forgive you, it dances in jubilation.

So We is not a choice anymore, not if you and I want to grow with one another. We unites us, increases our strength; it picks up our burden when you and I are ready to let it fall. The truth is that you and I would have given up long ago, but We won't let us. It is too wise. "Look into your hearts," it says. "What do you see? Not you and I, but only We."

ANGEL OF LIGHT

It's hard to see angels, although I've stared at their pictures for hours. Some people can see them without pictures, and they tell interesting tales. Guardian angels are all female, for instance, which didn't surprise me once I found out. A birth angel, recruited from the younger ranks, attends every baby when it appears, while another angel, older but not grim, helps the dying to leave this world without grief or pain.

You can pray to the angels and they will listen, but the best way to call them, I am told, is to laugh. Angels respond to delight, because that is what they're made of. In fact, when people's minds are clouded by anger or hatred, no angel can reach them.

Not all angels have wings – so the visionaries claim – but those who do can unfurl a span of golden feathers stretching over the entire world. If you had eyes that could look straight into the sun, you would see an overwhelming angel presiding there; a more serene one smiles out from the face of the moon.

Angels spend their entire lives, which are forever, spinning around the Creator's throne, singing His praise. People with keen ears have listened in. The harmonies of the angelic choir are incredibly complex, they say, but the rhythm is simple. "It's mostly march time," one eavesdropper affirmed. For some reason, that fact is almost the best I have learned so far.

After a while it got lonely hearing about angels you couldn't see for yourself. When an angel-watcher heard that, she was shocked. "Not see?" she said. "But you have an angel in you. Everybody does. I can see it right now, and I thought you could, too." "No," I said sadly, and I asked what it looked like. "Did it look like me?"

"Well, yes and no," the angel-watcher mysteriously answered. "It all depends on what you think you are. Your angel is a speck of light perched at the very center of your heart. It is smaller than an atom, but just wait. Once you get close to it, your angel will expand. The closer you come, the more it will grow, until finally, in a burst of light, you will see your angel in its true shape, and at that very instant, you will also see yourself."

So now I am looking for my angel all the time. I sit silently, turning my gaze inward. It wasn't long before I caught a glimpse of something. "Is that you, Angel, holding a candle?" One flicker and it was gone. Yet that was enough to set my heart wildly beating. Next time my angel will be waving a lamp, then holding a torch aloft, then lighting a bonfire.

That's what the angel-watcher promised, and now that I have caught sight of glory, I know enough to believe.

I SEARCHED FOR MY STAR

When I was little, I used to lie on my back in the grass at night. I began to tell one star from another and wished that one of them could be mine, like an imaginary friend.

First I picked the Pole Star, because it is the easiest for a child to find, once you know that the Big Dipper is about to catch it. But I wanted my star to be a moving star, and not such a constant one. Besides, the sailors at sea would be lost without the Pole Star to guide them.

Next I picked out two special stars in the heart of the Swan. All the other stars looked white – but these were bright blue and gold. They reminded me of twin jewels, but before I could choose, I stopped. They belonged to each other, and it wouldn't be fair to take just one.

Orion's belt caught my eye for a moment, but I'm not a hunter. I had better leave the Dog Star alone, too, with its nose pressed to the celestial trail and its tail thumping the sky.

Last of all I turned to my favorites, the Seven Sisters. To me they were like elegant ladies getting ready for a ball, wrapped in a gossamer blue cloud. But who has the heart to tear seven sisters apart?

My game taught me a lot about the night sky, but I was growing up. The whole idea of having my own star faded, and it was hard to remember if I had ever chosen one in the end. People began to tell me that the word "star" meant something quite different. I half believed them, then one night I was tossing in bed, hurt and worried. My heart felt heavy with troubles. Stumbling to my feet, I looked out the window. Thick clouds masked the midnight sky. No stars!

I trembled to think of a world without stars. No guide for the sailor to trust at sea, no jewels to dazzle our sense of beauty, no hunter pointing to the next horizon, no lovely ladies trailing perfume to heaven's ballroom. But all around the globe, the air is so dirty and the lights from cities are so bright that for some people few stars can be seen anymore. A generation of children may grow up seeing a blank sky and asking, "Did there used to be stars there?"

Let's give them back the sky and let's do it now – before it's too late. I'm going to search for my star until I find it. It's hidden in the drawer of innocence, wrapped in a scarf of wonder. I'll need a map to tell me which hole it should fill, and that will be a small one. But there are nearly five billion of us on earth, and we all need the sky. Find your star and throw it up to heaven. You still have it, don't you?

A CHILD IS A SONG

When children listen to music, they don't just listen. They melt into the melody and flow with the rhythm. Something inside starts to unfold its wings – soon the child and the music are one. I feel that way, too, in the presence of music, and my best moments of creativity have often been spent with children. When I am around them, music comes to me as easily as breathing.

Each song is a child I nourish and give my love to. But even if you have never written a song, your life is a song. How can it not be? In wave after wave, Nature caresses you – the rhythm of each dawn and each sunset is part of you, the falling rain touches your soul, and you see yourself in the clouds that are playing tag with the sun. To live is to be musical, starting with the blood dancing in your veins. Everything living has a rhythm. To feel each one, softly and attentively, brings out its music.

Do you feel your music?

Children do, but once we grow up, life becomes a burden and a chore, and the music grows fainter. Sometimes the heart is so heavy that we turn away from it and forget that its throbbing is the wisest message of life, a wordless message that says, "Live, be, move, rejoice – you are alive!" Without the heart's wise rhythm, we could not exist.

When I begin to feel a little tired or burdened, children revive me. I turn to them for new life, for new music. Two brown eyes look at me so deeply, so innocently, and inside I murmur, "This child is a song." It is so true and direct an experience that instantly I realize again, "I am a song also." I am back to myself once more.

CHILD OF INNOCENCE

Child of innocence, I miss your sunny days
We joyously frolicked in extended plays
Ever since you've left the scene
The streets are lonely, dark, and mean

Child of innocence, return to me now
With your simple smile show them how
This world once again can respond to your glance
And heartbeats flutter to the rhythm of your dance

Child of innocence, your elegance, your beauty
Beckons me now beyond the call of duty
Come fly with me far and above
Over the mountains in the land of love

Child of innocence, messenger of joy

You've touched my heart without a ploy
My soul is ablaze with a flagrant fire
To change this world is my deepest desire.

WILL YOU BE THERE?

Hold me like the river Jordan
And I will then say to thee
You are my friend
Carry me like you are my brother
Love me like a mother
Will you be there?

When weary tell me will you hold me?
When wrong, will you mold me?
When lost will you find me?
But they told me a man should be faithful
And walk when not able
And fight till the end
But I'm only human

Everyone's trying to control me
Seems that the world's got a role for me
I'm so confused
Will you show to me
You'll be there for me
And care enough to bear me?

Hold me, show me
Lay your head lowly
Gently and boldly
Carry me there
I'm only human

Hold me, show me
Lay your head lowly

Gently and boldly
Carry me there
I'm only human

Carry, carry
Carry me boldly
Gently and slowly
Carry me there
I'm only human

Knead me
Love me and feed me
Kiss me and free me
And I will feel blessed

Lonely
When I'm cold and lonely
And needing you only
Will you still care?
Will you be there?

Save me
Heal me and bathe me
Softly you say to me
I will be there
But will you be there?

Hold me
Hug me and shield me
Touch me and heal me
I know you care
But will you be there?

Lonely
When I'm cold and lonely
(I get lonely sometimes, I get lonely)
And needing you only

Will you still care?
Will you be there?

Carry
Carry me boldly
Gently and slowly
Carry me there

Knead me
Love me and feed me
Kiss me and free me
And I will be blessed

Call me
Save me and face me

Bless me and say to me
I will be there
I know you care

Save me
Heal me and bathe me
Softly you say to me
I will be there
But will you be there?

Feed me
Feed me and soothe me
When I'm lonely and hungry
Will you still share?
Will you still care?

Nurse me
Soothe me, don't leave me
When I'm hurting and bleeding

Bruised and bare
Will you still care?

Kiss me
Face me and kiss me
And when my heart is breaking
Will you still care?
Will you be here?

Lift me
Lift me up carefully
I'm weary and falling
I know you're there
But do you still care?

PART 2

MAGICAL CHILD

Magical child once felt a twinge
A faint recollection, a memory unhinged
In the colors, the forms, the hue
There seemed a mystery with a subtle clue
Behind the wind, the storm, the gale
Within the shroud, beyond the veil
Hidden from view in a wondrous pattern
There seemed a force that he could not fathom
Its music and cadence were playful and sweet
He danced in bliss to its throbbing beat
He did not mind either cold or heat
On the mountain high was his royal seat

Strangers came and scorned his joy
With ridicule and banter they tried to destroy
What in their minds was a skillful play
With cruel darts they tried to plunder
To suffocate and strangle his innocent wonder
Fighting hard, despite their blunder
Again and again to steal his thunder
Despite their attacks, they could not break
With all their barbs, they could not take
God's gift of love, which they could not fake
Not knowing his strength or what he sought to seek
They complained aloud and called him a freak

But the mysterious force just kept its hold
Magical child grew brave and bold
Diving deep into his soul
In exquisite ecstasy he discovered his role
In his Self was infinite scope
This mysterious force was mankind's hope
Piercing through that mask of Being
In that silence beyond all seeing
Was a field with a different story
A field of power, of awesome glory
With other children, if unfurled
Its tidal wave would change the world

Magical child was ready to bow
Sow the seed, pick up the plough
With effortless ease, without a sigh
Without a tear, without a cry
With silent perfection
Under God's direction
To sing together as one race
Stem the tide, transform this place

Magical children, don't worry how
Don't delay, this moment's now.

ARE YOU LISTENING?

Who am I?
Who are you?
Where did we come from?
Where are we going?
What's it all about?
Do you have the answers?

Immortality's my game
From Bliss I came
In Bliss I am sustained
To Bliss I return
If you don't know it now
It's a shame
Are you listening?

This body of mine
Is a flux of energy
In the river of time
Eons pass, ages come and go
I appear and disappear
Playing hide-and-seek
In the twinkling of an eye

I am the particle
I am the wave
Whirling at lightning speed
I am the fluctuation
That takes the lead
I am the Prince
I am the Knave
I am the doing
That is the deed
I am the galaxy, the void of space
In the Milky Way
I am the craze

I am the thinker, the thinking, the thought
I am the seeker, the seeking, the sought
I am the dewdrop, the sunshine, the storm
I am the phenomenon, the field, the form
I am the desert, the ocean, the sky
I am the Primeval Self
In you and I

Pure unbounded consciousness
Truth, existence, Bliss am I
In infinite expressions I come and go
Playing hide-and-seek
In the twinkling of an eye
But immortality's my game

Eons pass
Deep inside
I remain
Ever the same
From Bliss I came
In Bliss I am sustained

Join me in my dance
Please join me now
If you forget yourself
You'll never know how
This game is played
In the ocean bed of Eternity

Stop this agony of wishing
Play it out
Don't think, don't hesitate
Curving back within yourself
Just create...just create

Immortality's my game

From Bliss I came
In Bliss I'm sustained
To Bliss I return
If you don't know it now
It's a shame
Are you listening?

BREAKING FREE

All this hysteria, all this commotion
Time, space, energy are just a notion
What we have conceptualized we have created
All those loved, all those hated

Where is the beginning, where's the end
Time's arrow, so difficult to bend
Those broken promises, what they meant
Those love letters, never sent

ONCE WE WERE THERE

Before the beginning, before the violence
Before the anguish of the broken silence
A thousand longings, never uttered
Pangs of sorrow, brutally smothered

But I have chosen to break and be free
Cut those ties, so I can see
Those bonds that imprisoned me in memories of pain
Those judgments, interpretations that cluttered my brain

Those festering wounds that lingered have gone
In their place a new life has dawned

That lonely child, still clutching his toy
Has made his peace, discovered his joy

Where time is not, immortality's clear
Where love abounds, there is no fear
The child has grown to weave his magic
Left behind
His life of sorrow, once so tragic

He is now, ready to share
Ready to love, ready to care
Unfold his heart, with nothing to spare
Join him now, if you dare.

HEAVEN IS HERE

You and I were never separate
It's just an illusion
Wrought by the magical lens of
Perception

There is only one Wholeness
Only one Mind
We are like ripples
In the vast Ocean of Consciousness

Come, let us dance
The Dance of Creation
Let us celebrate
The Joy of Life

The birds, the bees
The infinite galaxies
Rivers, Mountains
Clouds and Valleys
Are all a pulsating pattern

Living, breathing
Alive with cosmic energy
Full of Life, of Joy
This Universe of Mine
Don't be afraid

To know who you are
You are much more
Than you ever imagined

You are the Sun
You are the Moon
You are the wildflower in bloom
You are the Life-throb
That pulsates, dances
From a speck of dust
To the most distant star

And you and I
Were never separate
It's just an illusion
Wrought by the magical lens of
Perception

Let us celebrate
The Joy of Life
Let us dance
The Dance of Creation

Curving back within ourselves
We create
Again and again
Endless cycles come and go
We rejoice
In the infinitude of Time

There never was a time
When I was not
Or you were not
There never will be a time
When we will cease to be

Infinite   Unbounded
In the Ocean of Consciousness
We are like ripples
In the Sea of Bliss

You and I were never separate
It's just an illusion
Wrought by the magical lens of
Perception

Heaven is Here
Right now is the moment
of Eternity
Don't fool yourself
Reclaim your Bliss

Once you were lost
But now you're home
In a nonlocal Universe
There is nowhere to go
From Here to Here
Is the Unbounded
Ocean of Consciousness
We are like ripples
In the Sea of Bliss

Come, let us dance
The Dance of Creation
Let us celebrate
The Joy of Life

And

You and I were never separate
It's just an illusion
Wrought by the magical lens of
Perception

Heaven is Here
Right now, this moment of Eternity
Don't fool yourself
Reclaim your Bliss

QUANTUM LEAP

I looked for you in hill and dale
I sought for you beyond the pale
I searched for you in every nook and cranny
My probing was at times uncanny
But everywhere I looked I found
I was just going round and round
In every storm, in every gale
I could hear your silent tale

You appeared wherever I went
In every taste, in every scent
I thought I was in a trance
In every quiver I felt your dance
In every sight I saw your glance
You were there, as if by chance

Even so, I have faltered
Despite the fact, my life has altered
All my doubts were struggles in vain
Of judgments made in memories of pain
Only now, by letting go
I can bask in your glow
No matter where I stray or flow
I see the splendor of your show

In every drama I am the actor
In every experience the timeless factor

In every dealing, every deed
You are there, as the seed
I know now, for I have seen
What could have happened could have been
There is no need to try so hard
For in your sleeve you hold the card
For every fortune, every fame
The Kingdom's here for us to claim
In every fire, every hearth
There's a spark gives new birth

To all those songs never sung
All those longings in hearts still young
Beyond all hearing, beyond all seeing
In the core of your Being
Is a field that spans infinity
Unbounded pure is the embryo of divinity
If we could for one moment BE
In an instant we would see
A world where no one has suffered or toiled
Of pristine beauty never soiled
Of sparkling waters, singing skies
Of hills and valleys where no one dies

That enchanted garden, that wondrous place
Where we once frolicked in times of grace
In ourselves a little deep
In that junkyard in that heap
Beneath that mound of guilt and sorrow
Is the splendor of another tomorrow
If you still have promises to keep
Just take that plunge, take that leap.

THAT ONE IN THE MIRROR

I wanted to change the world, so I got up one morning and looked in the mirror. That one looking back said, "There is not much time left. The earth is wracked with pain. Children are starving. Nations remain divided by mistrust and hatred. Everywhere the air and water have been fouled almost beyond help. Do something!"

That one in the mirror felt very angry and desperate. Everything looked like a mess, a tragedy, a disaster. I decided he must be right. Didn't I feel terrible about these things, too, just like him? The planet was being used up and thrown away. Imagining earthly life just one generation from now made me feel panicky.

It was not hard to find the good people who wanted to solve the earth's problems. As I listened to their solutions, I thought, "There is so much good will here, so much concern." At night before going to bed, that one in the mirror looked back at me seriously, "Now we'll get somewhere," he declared. "If everybody does their part."

But everybody didn't do their part. Some did, but were they stopping the tide? Were pain, starvation, hatred, and pollution about to be solved? Wishing wouldn't make it so – I knew that. When I woke up the next morning, that one in the mirror looked confused. "Maybe it's hopeless," he whispered. Then a sly look came into his eyes, and he shrugged. "But you and I will survive. At least we are doing all right."

I felt strange when he said that. There was something very wrong here. A faint suspicion came to me, one that had never dawned so clearly before. What if that one in the mirror isn't me? He feels separate. He sees problems "out there" to be solved. Maybe they will be, maybe they won't. He'll get along. But I don't feel that way – those problems aren't "out there," not really. I feel them inside me. A child crying in Ethiopia, a sea gull struggling pathetically in an oil spill, a mountain gorilla being mercilessly hunted, a teenage soldier trembling with terror when he hears the planes fly over : Aren't these happening in me when I see and hear about them?

The next time I looked in the mirror, that one looking back had started to fade. It was only an image after all. It showed me a solitary person enclosed in a neat package of skin and bones. "Did I once think you were me?" I began to wonder. I am not so separate and afraid. The pain of life touches me, but the joy of life is so much stronger. And it alone will heal. Life is the healer of life, and the most I can do for the earth is to be its loving child.

That one in the mirror winced and squirmed. He hadn't thought so much about love. Seeing "problems" was much easier, because love means complete self-honesty. Ouch!

"Oh, friend," I whispered to him, "do you think anything can solve problems without love?" That one in the mirror wasn't sure. Being alone for so long, not trusting others and being trusted by others, it tended to detach itself from the reality of life. "Is love more real than pain?" he asked.

"I can't promise that it is. But it might be. Let's discover," I said. I touched the mirror with a grin. "Let's not be alone again. Will you be my partner? I hear a dance starting up. Come." That one in the mirror smiled shyly. He was realizing that we could be best friends. We could be more peaceful, more loving, more honest with each other every day.

Would that change the world? I think it will, because Mother Earth wants us to be happy and to love her as we tend her needs. She needs fearless people on her side, whose courage comes from being part of her, like a baby who is brave enough to walk because Mother is holding out her arms to catch him. When that one in the mirror is full of love for me and for him, there is no room for fear. When we were afraid and panicky, we stopped loving this life of ours and this earth. We disconnected. Yet how can anybody rush to help the earth if they feel disconnected? Perhaps the earth is telling us what she wants, and by not listening, we fall back on our own fear and panic.

One thing I know: I never feel alone when I am earth's child. I do not have to cling to my personal survival as long as I realize, day by day, that all of life is in me. The children and their pain; the children and their joy. The ocean swelling under the sun; the ocean weeping with black oil. The animals hunted in fear; the animals bursting with the sheer joy of being alive.

This sense of "the world in me" is how I always want to feel. That one in the mirror has his doubts sometimes. So I am tender with him. Every morning I touch the mirror and whisper, "Oh, friend, I hear a dance. Will you be my partner? Come."

LOOK AGAIN, BABY SEAL

One of the most touching nature photographs is of a baby fur seal lying on the ice alone. I'm sure you have seen it – the picture seems to be all eyes, the trusting dark eyes of a small animal gazing up at the camera and into your heart. When I first looked at them, the eyes asked, "Are you going to hurt me?" I knew the answer was yes, because thousands of baby seals were being killed every year.

Many people were touched by one baby seal's helplessness. They gave money to save the seals, and public awareness started to shift. As I returned to the picture, those two wide eyes began to say something different. Now they asked, "Do you know me?" This time I didn't feel so much heartache as when I felt the violence man inflicts upon animals. But I realized that there was still a big gap. How much did I really know about life on earth? What responsibility did I feel for creatures outside my little space? How could I lead my life so that every cell of living matter was also benefited?

Everyone who began to wonder about these things found, I think, that their feelings were shifting away from fear toward more closeness with life as a whole. The beauty and wonder of life began to seem very personal; the possibility of making the planet a garden for all of us to grow in began to dawn. I looked into the eyes of the baby seal, and for the first time they smiled. "Thank you," they said. "You have given me hope."

Is that enough? Hope is such a beautiful word, but it often seems very fragile. Life is still being needlessly hurt and destroyed. The image of one baby seal alone on the ice or one baby girl orphaned in war is still frightening in its helplessness. I realized that nothing would finally save life on earth but trust in life itself, in its power to heal, in its ability to survive our mistakes and welcome us back when we learn to correct those mistakes.

With these thoughts in my heart, I looked at the picture again. The seal's eyes seemed much deeper now, and I saw something in them that I had missed before: unconquerable strength. "You have not hurt me," they said. "I am not one baby alone. I am life, and life can never be killed. It is the power that brought me forth from the emptiness of space; it cared for me and nourished my existence against all dangers. I am safe because I am that power. And so are you. Be with me, and let us feel the power of life together, as one creature here on earth."

Baby seal, forgive us. Look at us again and again to see how we are doing. Those men who raise their clubs over you are also fathers and brothers and sons. They have loved and cared for others. One day they will extend that love to you. Be sure of it and trust.

THE DREAM CONTINUES ...

照片所属
(Photo credits)

迪利普·梅塔
(Dilip Mehta)

山姆·爱默生
(Sam Emerson)

约纳桑·埃克斯利
(Jonathan Exley)

格列格·戈尔曼
(Greg Gorman)

绘画作者
(Paintings by)

大卫·诺尔达尔
(David Nordahl)

奈特·吉奥尔吉奥
(Nate Giorgio)

特别感谢
(Special thanks to)

山姆·爱默生
(Sam Emerson)